THE WIL

THE WILD

Esther Freud

HAMISH HAMILTON · LONDON

HAMISH HAMILTON LTD

Published by the Penguin Group
Penguin Books Ltd, 27 Wrights Lane, London w8 5TZ, England
Penguin Putnam Inc., 375 Hudson Street, New York, New York 10014, USA
Penguin Books Australia Ltd, Ringwood, Victoria, Australia
Penguin Books Canada Ltd, 10 Alcorn Avenue, Toronto, Ontario,
Canada M4V 3B2
Penguin Books (NZ) Ltd, Private Bag 102902, NSMC, Auckland,
New Zealand

Penguin Books Ltd, Registered Offices: Harmondsworth, Middlesex, England

First published 2000
1 3 5 7 9 10 8 6 4 2

Phototypeset in Monotype Plantin Light by Intype London Ltd

Printed in Great Britain by Clays Ltd, St Ives plc

A CIP catalogue record for this book is available from the British Library

ISBN 0-241-14086-2

For David, Albie
and Anna Kitty

THE WILD

Esther Freud

William could hear them in the sudden stillness, the scuffle of the children's feet, their clumsiness as the workshop door swung open and then shut. There was a high chime as a trowel bounced on the path, and the cat flap in the loose panel of the door rattled as it slammed into the wall.

'Daddy!' they called as they streamed through from the lawn. 'William, where are you?' They raced past the chicken shed, and along the moulded track to where the caravan, fresh and brightly painted, was nestled in the gloom.

'William, what is it?' Francine had run out of the kitchen, her hands still wringing from the washing up. 'William . . . what's happening?' Her long skirt skimmed the ground, and the chickens clucked around her in the hope of food. She stood there, unsure, straining past him into the caravan to see, and from where William stood he could feel her body trembling.

'You'd better get an ambulance,' he told her, and just as she was about to rush forward, he blocked her view into the caravan's one room. 'Quickly now Francine, there's been an accident here.'

'Should I run down to the phonebox?' She was like a child herself now, her speckled eyes staring into his, and irritated and afraid for her, he shouted, 'No, go next door. Quickly. Just go next door and call.'

Francine ran, her skirt pulled up into her hand, and he could see just from the way her hair stood up electric on her neck that she was too afraid to ask.

'Stay back now,' he told the children, and he realized he was still holding the gun. 'Stay back.' He shut his eyes against their open stares, all four of them, their faces tilted up in shock, and in one swift movement he pulled his shirt off over his head. He squashed it into a ball and kneeling on the wooden floor he pressed it against the child's body to try and stop the blood. 'Shhh now,' he said, and over the drum of his own heart he felt with his fingers for a pulse.

Dear Dad,

We're living in a really brilliant house. It's got a garden with a badminton net and another one for vegetables and William says we can all have a garden of our own down by the garage. William is building it himself. (The garage.) Also there's the wild which is full of mud and trees and William says he'll clear it out and build a chicken coop. He thinks that might be my job, feeding the chickens. I hope so. I'm very well. Jake sends his love. (He says he'll write when he's not in a bad mood.)

How are you? I'm very well.

Love Tess

A week later Tess received a letter back. Not just a card for her and Jake, but an envelope, a rich cream envelope with her name dented into it in ink.

Dear Tess,

I'm glad to hear that you're so well. William sounds like quite a fellow. Maybe I should come and visit, see the garage for myself?

Love Dad

They were having breakfast and William was making toast while Francine cleared away the muesli dishes. It was William's idea that they all eat together, Jake and Tess and his three daughters – all eat the same thing, at the same time, at every meal. Until last week they'd eaten

3

when they felt like it, especially in the mornings, and Jake in particular was having trouble adjusting to these rules. Tess glanced at William as he toasted bread on the hotplate of the Rayburn, gently wrapping each slice in a fold of tea towel until he had a hot thick stack.

'Me first for toast.' Sandy was William's youngest daughter and still needed jam spreading for her with someone else's knife.

'She's spoilt.' Doon kicked her under the table and they scowled at each other and stuck out their tongues.

'Mum,' Tess called, but Francine was running water into the sink. William handed the hot parcel of toast to Honour, who took a piece daintily, and handed it on to Jake.

'Thanks, Honour,' Jake said in a nasty high-up voice. Honour was in Jake's class at school and he couldn't see why suddenly, just because William Strachan had rented them two rooms, he and Honour were expected to be friends.

'Mum,' Tess called over the noise. 'Dad says he might come and visit us here.'

Jake looked up, honey dripping from his knife. 'Really?'

Francine smiled. She picked the letter up and, still smiling, nodded over it. 'How nice.' But Tess could tell she didn't think for one minute it was true.

'Pass it here,' Jake ordered and Francine hovered between her children's outstretched hands. 'Me,' Jake demanded and Francine edged it his way.

William took his seat at the other end of the table and Sandy climbed on to his knee. 'Daddy . . .'

'What?' He turned his good ear towards her. The other had been injured in an accident, something that involved a car explosion or a gun.

'Nothing.' She snuggled down.

William used his long arms to butter toast around her. 'Today,' he said, his mouth full, 'we're going to cut down a tree.'

'Hurray!' Doon and Sandy shouted. 'Hurray!' Tess joined in a second too late. She wasn't used to such adventures. Honour sat up straighter as if in preparation for the most responsible of tasks, and even Jake couldn't help but look intrigued.

'I'm going to need help from Jake, and from all you girls.' William smiled around the table and crinkled his eyes to show he meant Francine as well. 'We'll drive up on to the forest, and find the right kind of tree, and then . . .' – his voice grew serious – 'you'll have to be very careful while I use the chainsaw.'

'Are you allowed to do that?' Francine asked. 'Just wander around cutting down trees?'

William put his head to one side, pointing to his deaf ear, so that she had to ask the question twice. 'Of course.' He thumped the table. Sandy bounced into the air. 'Forestry rights come with the house. We'll bring in enough firewood to see us through the winter.' And he strode off to load the chainsaw into the van.

5

The Ashdown Forest was thick with bracken, fraying and unfurling red, but the wide soft lanes that ran up to the golf-course were still green.

'There aren't many trees for a forest,' Honour said, sitting in the front between Francine and William while Jake was crouched by the back doors, as far away as he could get.

'I know the man to ask.' William drove the van as if it were a ship, rollicking over the humps and mounds as he steered it through a shiny copse of birch.

'Look, a little house.' Doon craned to see. 'All hidden away.' And there it was, in a sudden valley, a crumbling old house that poked out of the earth.

William pulled on the brake and swung open the door.

'Who lives there?' They were out now and Tess was holding tight on to her mother's hand. It was the kind of house that should be haunted, with a crooked front gate and a garden fence all caving in. There were rows of Brussels sprouts and cabbages garlanded with thin white plastic bags. Bottle tops were strung in twittering lines. There was even a broom scarecrow, its whole face bristled with a beard.

William signalled for everyone to be quiet. 'Mr Jenkin-shaw?' he called towards the house, and as they waited the top half of the white front door opened and an old man leaned out. 'Morning,' he said, and all five children froze right where they were. They were so silent the air hummed high around them, but they still didn't hear a word of what was said.

'What happened to him?' They danced round William. 'What happened?' Tess shook her arms and legs and writhed against the grass, covering her face and wondering what it would be like to live without a nose. 'What happened? Arrrggghhhh! Yuk!' Mr Jenkinshaw was safe behind his stable door. 'Heebie geebie yikes!' The thought of him was like itching with nits.

'Calm down, the lot of you!' William was taking in his information, making calculations and scouting round for trees. 'Ssshh now.' But Francine wondered aloud if Mr Jenkinshaw's nose was the result of syphilis, or an injury from the war.

'Blown off, you mean?' Jake gasped and they all writhed and rolled some more, feeling strange electric tingles run up through their legs.

They drove the van up on to a shrubby plateau and William carried the chainsaw towards a tall thin ash. There was ivy growing up into its branches and he pointed this out as a sign that eventually the tree was going to die.

'Stand back, the lot of you!' William strained with one foot on the chainsaw, his face reddening a shade darker with each pull.

Tess watched the sinews of his arm, veins dark against white skin as he stretched the string and tried to catch it as it ticked. Jake sniggered and Tess glowered at him, hoping and hoping that the next time William tried he'd burst the chainsaw into life. 'Hurray!!' Sandy cheered when the machine finally caught and roared and William made her squeal away by threatening to brandish it against her long loose hair.

The noise it made was horrible, whining and screaming into wood, and then as if by magic, just at the point William had planned, the tree crashed down into the ferns. William switched off the chainsaw and shouted for them to gather round. 'It's all to do with angles,' he said, 'working out the exact direction a tree should fall.' He stopped for a moment to take his jacket off.

'How do you know these things?' Francine was flushed, her eyes hot, her lashes melting.

William shrugged and flicked the hair back from his face. 'Just wait till you taste my ravioli,' he winked, flipping his tongue around the word. Jake turned in disgust and walked away.

'Jake!' Tess ran after him, but just then the chainsaw started up again and William began slicing the thin tree into logs. Honour, Doon and Sandy formed a queue. They waited, well trained, to carry each log as it came and heave it through the back doors of the van. William cut specially small ones for Sandy, kindling, they would have to be, and he formed Doon and Tess into a team so that with their combined strength they could get one good log off the ground. Jake, Honour and Francine were the best workers and William stopped after a while to tell them so. He winked at Jake, man to man, and used the opportunity to take off his shirt. His back was white and long and his stomach when he bent down was ridged in a hard knot over his belt. There was a thin white scar curled over his left side and Tess wondered if it was caused by the same explosion that had shot the sound out of his ear.

The next day Tess wrote back to her father. She imagined him in his half-empty, bare-boarded flat where a bath stood alone in the middle of the floor. He lived there with Georgina, a woman as beautiful as pearls, and once when Tess and Jake were visiting she saw her father put his hand under Georgina's skirt. Georgina was in the kitchen warming up spaghetti hoops, and she didn't blush or struggle, but simply moved away to fetch two plates.

Dear Dad,

It would be really great if you did come and visit. I could show you the tallest tree in the wild. I've been banging nails into it so that I can climb up to where the branches start. William might have made the chicken coop by then. I hope so, although we'll have to be careful about foxes.
Love Tess

It was the first week in September and school was starting up again. William was starting school as well. 'I'll be able to keep an eye on you,' he joked, looking at the

9

five of them seated round the table, but in fact he would be teaching in the Upper School and no one was old enough for his class. Jake and Honour were eleven, Tess was nine, and Doon and Sandy were seven and four. Sandy was still in Kindergarten. Upper School didn't start until you were fourteen, but now that William was teaching Tess couldn't wait till she was there.

Everything was going to be different for them this year. For one thing, they'd drive to school with William in his van, and wouldn't have to wait out on the road for a lift. In the last house they'd lived, at Oakridge, a mile further away along the Oakfield Rd, they'd been picked up by a family called Biggs who drove right past their gate. They'd wait there every morning, betting on the cars, and every single morning they'd worried that they'd come out too late. At first Francine would wait with them, but often she had cleaning jobs that started before nine, and she would take the bus that stopped especially for her just before the bend. Sometimes Odin followed them out on to the road and they had to shoo him back when the Biggs' car eventually drew up. Odin was Jake's cat. He was named after the most powerful of all the Norse gods. Really he should have been called Thor, who was an angry god, but the name Odin carried better on the wind, and every night Jake had to stand by the back door and call and call him in for supper. Odin was ferocious. He had claws like iron spikes and his eyes and ears were orange. He had been a present on Jake's seventh birthday, and from the moment he saw his pointy ears sticking out of a crepe-paper box he fell in love with him.

It was partly because of Odin that they'd had to move away from Oakridge. The Wilkses, whose two ground-floor rooms they rented, had had enough of him. He'd gashed Mrs Wilks's boyfriend Ken, and then one day, running at great speed along a corridor, he'd collided with Imelda. Imelda was Mrs Wilks's youngest girl, and instead of skirting round her, he'd run straight up her front and, using her head as a propeller, he'd leapt from there on to the stairs. It made Tess laugh hard every time she thought of it, but she did feel bad when even a week later she saw that Imelda still had red welts under her fringe.

William cooked porridge on the first morning of term.

'Porridge!' Jake was appalled, and even Honour dabbed at it half-hearted with her spoon.

'It's delicious,' William insisted, and he sprinkled his with salt.

'Mum?' Jake looked to her for help, but she simply pushed a pot of honey in his direction and, as if to lure him on, swallowed down a thick white glutinous spoonful.

For special treats Jake and Tess used to have cheese on toast for breakfast. It was their favourite food and halfway through the toasting Francine would pull out the grill and splash vinegar over the melting cheese. It gave it an extra delicious taste like the Welsh rarebit served at Miriam's cafe, and they'd sit up in bed, the three of them, and eat it.

Jake stood up and moved towards the larder. He disappeared inside, re-emerging after a second with a tin of golden syrup, an old blackening tin that had made the move with them, and using the edge of his knife he prised off the lid. He dipped a teaspoon into it, and with the thick mass clinging, he wrote his name in gold across the porridge skin. 'That's better,' he said, and he looked hard-eyed in William's direction.

Jake had chosen his place at the end of the table, as far away from William as he could get. William was the only one who had a chair. The others squeezed on to wooden benches, three on either side, and on that first evening of the day that they'd moved in, their places had been set. Tess had marked out her seat beside Sandy, her back towards the door, so that when Sandy inevitably clambered on to her father's lap, it was she who was beside him. She could slide along the bench until she felt the heat of his white arm, and she would sit and snuggle close to his good ear.

William clutched his school bag tightly. 'Time to go,' he shouted, and he realized with suprise that he was nervous. In Aberdeen he'd taught in schools where most children had false teeth by the age of twelve. Small boys braved whole winters in acrylic shirts, and even the girls despised him for refusing to beat them with the cane. He'd tried to interest them in History, give them a pride in who they were. He'd filled the gaps in the curriculum with stories of Red Indians, Aboriginals, and the battles of the Picts, but they'd only sneered at him and called him Geek and Pansy, and asked why, if he was really Scottish, he talked just like the Queen.

'I dae nae talk like the Queen.' He'd tried to make a joke of it, but his chest was ready to cave in. 'I was born not two miles from here, in fact.' And he cursed his parents for moving him to Surrey so that he and his brother might 'get on'.

'You look as if you might even have Red Indian blood,' Felicity had told him, her fingers catching in his corn-syrup hair. 'A blond Red Indian,' she'd laughed. But that was long ago when they were at Aberdeen University, the bump that was to be Honour swelling out the soft line of her waist.

'Good luck today.' It was Francine, smiling at him, helping Tess on with her coat. 'I'll see you later.' He wondered if she'd noticed how he'd had his hair cut in a smart slope around his head.

Jake clanked open the back door of the van. An old rug had been stretched across the floor, and the wood chips cleared away. He sat down on the raised metal of the wheel arch and Honour, her pale glasses pressed tight against her face, climbed in and took the other. Doon and

Sandy slipped into the front, pinching and prodding each other across the torn foam of the black plastic seat. Tess tried her luck and squeezed in after them, pressing herself between Doon and the door so that she had to stand up sideways to slam it shut.

'Into the back now, Tess. Two's the limit.' William swung in, and sheepishly she climbed over the seat.

Tess sat in the spare tyre, looking up occasionally at the wide windshield of sky, but even without a view she knew every turn and bump, every dip and pause that led towards the village of Twelve Ashes. She closed her eyes and felt the van swerve, take the bend beyond the church and trundle up the last hill towards their school.

George House school was different. Tess knew this because no one from Twelve Ashes really talked to the children who went there, and sometimes when she caught the bus home the driver snarled and made a fuss when she didn't have exactly the right change. But the strangest thing about their school was the way that everything was sloped. The buildings, the signposts and the writing, everything was angled at a tilt. It was part of George House philosophy that no one should see corners, which meant the doors to the main building were curved over at the top and each wooden window frame was made of eight sides. Letters of the alphabet were shaded and bent, and all the signposts were chiselled into wood. There wasn't any uniform, apart from a ban on plimsolls or

clogs, but between Michaelmas and Easter no girl was to
be seen in ankle socks, no boy in shorts, and it was often
mentioned that the British habit of sending children out
in winter with bare, frozen legs was responsible for many
of the ills of later life. And then, of course, no one wore
glasses. No one except Honour, that was, but then Honour
was still new. All children with weak eyesight were sent to
the school nurse for special exercises, and the year before,
for two and a half terms, Tess had been ordered to throw
rods.

'Come in,' Miss Glot had called floatily, and as soon as
Tess was inside the First Aid hut a copper rod was put
into her hand. The rod was light and cool, warming
quickly in her palm, and the nurse showed her how to
throw it in a perfect arc across the room. At first Miss
Glot simply caught the rod and threw it back to her, but
soon she took up a rod of her own, rolling it out along her
fingers so that it flew like fire through the room. Miss Glot
wore grey eurythmy shoes with an elasticated T, and if
Tess wobbled and let her rod lunge, Miss Glot would
have to leap on her short legs to catch it. But soon Tess
was drawn into a rhythm. The two rods arced up and
passed each other so that she and Miss Glot were joined
together in a syrupy ring of movement, the rods flying
out and dipping down into their outstretched hands, the
smell of copper rising as their fingers heated up. Flinging
and whirring, flinging and whirring, the muscles in their
eyes worked back and forth. It was always a surprise when

Miss Glot slowed the movement, drawing the rods to an eventual halt. 'You can go now, Tess,' Miss Glot would say kindly, as the bell rang for the end of break, and dizzily Tess would find herself outside.

'Wouldn't it be funny,' Jake had said at supper just the other night, 'if while you were doing those exercises for your sight, a rod flew and poked out your eye.' He'd started laughing, choking so hard that a parsnip chip flew out of his mouth. Francine's face broke into a smile, and Tess began to giggle, but William seemed not to have heard and instead caused an uproar by stealing the sausage from Sandy's plate.

'Look at that bird on the window-sill,' he'd said, and when she turned back she found the sausage gone. 'No,' she wailed, but there was delight in her eyes and it was clear from the expectant faces of the others that this was a trick he'd played on her before.

This year Jake's classroom was going to be purple. Purple for Class Six. Blue for Five, green for Four, yellow for Three, and for Classes Two and One a mottled wash of pink. Tess could see her Class Four green through the window as she passed, newly painted in a sea-sponge press of swirls, and there beside the blackboard was her own class teacher, Mr Paul. She raced through the main hall, past the carved stone sculpture of St George wrestling with a snake, and slid along the corridor. *Mr Paul, Mr Paul*; in her mind's eye she flew into his arms.

'Mr Paul?' she said instead, and he half-turned to her and smiled. He was drawing a picture on the blackboard of a range of mountains streaked with sun. Below the mountains lay a giant, and below the giant a raging, flaming land of fire and gore.

'Hello,' Tess said, and she wanted to take hold of his square hand and tell him about William. About the chainsaw and the ravioli, and how William sang songs and accompanied himself with a guitar. But they stood there, smiling, shy after an endless summer break, and turning back he continued shading rays of light streaking down from the blackboard's chalky edge. Tess imagined he'd been standing there all holiday, chalking and shading to get the colours right.

Mr Paul had his own daughter, a pale girl in the class above, and when Tess saw her in the playground she wondered if she minded not being in his class. It was true she saw her father in the evenings and over the weekend, but Tess was with him every morning, heard the stories he made up out of everything he knew, and she'd had him to herself since she was six.

'Mum, I mean Mr Paul . . .' Tess said, sidling close, but just then a stream of other children pressed in, and she rushed off to choose her desk.

★

'So?' William asked at supper. 'How was your first day?' He looked around the table at the five children, the first strands of spaghetti slooped into their mouths. 'Honour?'

'Fine.' She kept her eyes on her plate and Jake glanced at the narrow line of her high shoulders pressed towards each ear.

'Jake?' William bent forward, waiting to hear the worst, but Jake looked clear into his eyes and said it had been good. 'We're doing woodwork. And I'm making a bowl.'

'That's great.'

'Yes, a pudding bowl,' he said, dipping his chin with mirth, and he glanced meaningfully at William's bright blond round of hair.

'At Kindergarten,' Sandy piped up, 'we sang lots of songs.' She started singing one into her father's ear. 'And he played upon a ladle, a ladle, a ladle, and he played upon a ladle and his name was Aikin Drum.'

'And how about you, Doon?' William asked, serious, as if there might be a reason why she should need particularly to be asked. Doon told them about her teacher Miss Bibeen, and how she'd been to visit her mother in Japan. Doon stopped on the word 'mother' with a little start and looked up, not sure if she was allowed to carry on. 'She told us about it for the whole mainlesson,' she said then, and biting her lip she stared hard at her food.

Tess waited, sucking up spaghetti, slowing each mouthful for her turn, longing to tell how they'd started hearing the Norse Myths, learning about Ginnungagap and the creation of the world, and how soon she'd have her very own stories about Odin, Loki and Thor. But William got up to fill the water jug and without seeming to see her he began to explain that there was a school play he wanted to direct. 'Greek tragedy,' he said. 'We'll perform it in the round, turn the gym into an amphitheatre. Bring some real drama into the school.'

'Just help yourself to fruit,' Francine called, as benches clattered and feet dropped to the floor and she started clearing dishes for the washing up.

Dear Dad,

Can I tell you about Ginnungagap?

First there was a Realm called Muspell. No one could endure it or would want to, except those born into it. Then there was Niflheim. Packed with ice and snow. And between these two Realms stretched a huge emptiness. Ginnungagap.

But then out of the ice and snow came the first Frost Giant. His name was Ymir. Ymir was evil, and while he slept he began to sweat. A man and woman grew out of the sweat under his left armpit, and one of his legs fathered a son with the other leg. Ymir was the forefather of all the Frost Giants.

How are you? I hope you're well. William says the garage is going to have to wait until the spring.

Love Tess

*

'Mum . . .' Tess climbed on to Francine's high bed, whistling for Odin to follow and curl against her knees.

'Yes,' Francine said, keeping both eyes on her book.

'It's not fair . . .'

'What's not?'

Tess hesitated. She was too ashamed to say. 'Jake's got the top bunk again,' she said instead.

'I know.' Francine glanced towards the door where Jake was pasting a poster of a leopard, drooling and ferocious, over one magnolia wall. There were lions there already and a cheetah, but he'd promised to leave Tess one oblong empty square. 'What will you put up?'

Tess didn't know. She had her treasures laid out on the window-sill. There was a tiny glass bottle, one earring, and a half-eaten sugar pig. The pig had been her father's. Tess had come across it, abandoned and forgotten in the debris of his desk. She'd picked it up, stared at it, crooked and warmed it in her palm, and thought how he must have had it since he was a boy. Eventually he'd noticed and asked if she'd like to take it home.

'Thank you, yes, if you're sure . . .'

And then that evening Jake had bitten off its head.

'No,' Tess wailed, and through her sobs she explained the pig was an antique.

'No wonder it tastes so disgusting!' Jake snarled, pink splinters dribbling on his chin. 'I think I might be sick,' and he threw the remains on to her lap.

Francine tried to Sellotape it back together, a jagged strip around its neck and leg, and she put it on Tess's treasure shelf, propped between an eggcup and a three-legged silver box.

'How do you know Dad had it all those years?' Jake asked that night, leaning down, draped like a bat over his bunk. 'How do you know?' But Tess pretended to be asleep.

Francine had a downstairs bedroom next to Tess and Jake in the extension William had built on to the house. The extension also had a bathroom and a laundry room, and he'd used the oldest, pinkest bricks so that it would look as if it had always been there. But really it still looked like Lego, welded on, and as soon as you opened the door out of the kitchen it smelled brand-new of damp and dust and tiles. Francine's room was so small there was no space for a bed. 'You think that now,' William had said when they came to look at their new home, 'but wait till you see what I have planned.' And it was true that by the time they moved in there was the skeleton of a fairy bed, snug between two walls. The frame was high, with a rail for curtains, and there were cupboards underneath to save on space.

'I got carried away,' William said, and he explained that he was using a fretsaw to curlicue the frame. 'A bed from the Arabian Nights,' he said, and while he was adding the final touches, Francine slept on cushions in the sitting room, using the mouth of the fireplace like a cave.

One night Tess woke, cold and wet, and went in search of her. 'Mum.' She peered into the shadows. 'Mum.' But her eyes had cleared to find she wasn't there. She'd had to get a towel and put it over the wet patch of the sheet herself, and keeping her knees high she'd gone shivering back to sleep.

'It's just because you're in a new place,' Francine told her when she found the rolled-up bedding in a corner of the room, and they smiled at each other, prepared to hope that this was true.

'Don't say anything . . .' Tess looked at her, but instead of nodding as she always did, Francine frowned, distracted, as if she wasn't sure.

'Mum!' Tess surged forward in terror.

'Don't worry,' Francine pressed her hand. 'Don't worry, I won't tell.'

William leant over the Rayburn, his face reflected, crooked in the silver hood. He pressed down on the rail and sighed. Francine was running water into the sink. From upstairs he could hear Honour practising her violin, lilting and catching on the exact same phrase, while Doon and Sandy bickered in their room. 'Daddeeeee . . .' They wanted him to go upstairs and sort it out and William wondered how long it was since they'd got on. There was a clatter and a prolonged wail, and then suddenly a silent breeze of peace. William began polishing the Rayburn. He used a small rag of oil and savoured the bitter scorching smell.

'Mum.' It was Tess. She was cross and she stamped over to her mother and stretched up to whisper in her ear.

'Don't worry . . . just leave it.' Francine was firm and Tess began to whine. 'Oh Muuummm . . .' William watched her irritably, her straggly hair, her awkward body, her plump legs and her tummy, rounded like a horse. She looked over at him suddenly as if he might want to help. William turned back to the polishing. He could feel her eyes, round and dark and hopeful, and he thought how her own father avoided that dark stare by simply paying money into an account. That could have been me. Living a high single life with cars and girls. But he knew he would have made almost any sacrifice to win that last bitter battle with his wife.

Mr Paul stood before the blackboard on which THE NORSE MYTHS was written in huge letters that shaded from purple through to blue. 'Burning ice, biting flame,' he said, 'that is how life began.' Tess trembled in her seat as Mr Paul's face paled with his own storytelling zeal. He didn't stand behind his desk but walked very slowly up and down in front of the class.

'As more of the ice on Ginnungagap melted, the fluid took the form of a cow. She was called Audumla. Ymir

23

fed off the four rivers of milk that coursed from her teats, and Audumla fed off the ice itself. She licked the salty blocks and by the evening of the first day a man's hair had come out of the ice. Audumla licked more and by the evening of the second day a man's head had appeared. Audumla licked again and by the evening of the third day the whole man had come. His name was Buri.'

Tess closed her eyes and tried to imagine Buri, but as if reading her thoughts Mr Paul went on. 'Buri was tall and strong and good-looking. In time he had a son called Bor and Bor married the daughter of a frost giant. Her name was Bestla and she mothered three children. The first was Odin, the second Vili, and the third was Ve.

'The three sons of Bor did not like Ymir and his gang of unruly frost giants, and soon they began to hate them. At last they attacked Ymir and killed him. His wounds were like springs, so much blood streamed from them and so fast that the flood drowned all the frost giants except Bergelmir and his wife, who stepped into their boat, and rode off on a tide of gore.'

'A bit like Noah?' Tess asked.

'Odin and his brothers took the body of the dead frost giant and carted it to the middle of Ginnungagap to form the world. They made the earth from Ymir's flesh and the mountains from his unbroken bones. From his teeth and jaws and the fragments of his shattered bones they made rocks and boulders and stones.

'Odin, Vili and Ve used the welter of blood to make land-locked lakes and to make the sea. After they had formed the earth, they laid the rocking ocean in a ring right round it. And it is so wide that most men would dismiss the very idea of crossing it. Then the three brothers raised Ymir's skull and made the sky from it and placed it so that its four corners reached to the ends of the earth. They set a dwarf under each corner and their names are East, West, North and South. Then Odin and Vili and Ve seized on the sparks and glowing embers from the southern realm of Muspell and called them sun and moon and stars. They put them high in Ginnungagap to light heaven above and earth below. In this way the brothers gave each star its proper place.

'The sons of Bor used Ymir's brains as well. They flung them up into the air and turned them into every kind of cloud.' Mr Paul rolled the blackboard to show the brains, white froth in a sea of blue, and he rolled and rolled to show how he'd shaded out every scrap of black.

William wanted everyone to think what they should call the house. Before he'd found it and started building, it hadn't been a house at all but an old bakery. There was a fireplace where the ovens used to be, big enough to sit inside, and above it was an enormous chimney. There was no proper upstairs, and The garden, even where the lawn was now, was wild.

'I wish I'd seen it then,' Tess said, and Sandy looked all pleased.

'I saw it,' she said. 'I saw it then.'

'Come on, girls,' William called. 'I want you all to think.'

'Honeysuckle cottage.' Doon's hand shot up.

William frowned. 'There isn't any honeysuckle.'

'We could plant some.' Tess agreed with Doon. It was a perfect name.

'How about The Cake House?' Honour said.

'Very clever,' William approved.

'Or Cheery Bricks?' Jake smiled.

Francine laughed.

'Now Jake,' William said. 'Let's be serious.'

'Cheery pricks,' Jake muttered just under his breath, and William swerved his eyes.

'How about . . .' – he leant his arms on the table – 'How about The Wild?'

'That's brilliant!' his children clamoured. 'The Wild!'

'You don't think just The Bakery?' Francine suggested. After all, it was the way their letters reached them now.

'Boring Francine, boring.' William waved his hands. 'The Wild.'

Suddenly the girls were whooping and hallooing, caught up in the excitement of the name. 'The Wild, The Wild,' they cried. 'We want The Wild.'

★

The estate of Laurel Hill was tranquil and maintained. There were rhododendron bushes and variegated shrubs and most of the inhabitants were retired or commuted to London for their work.

A curved road wound through the estate. It started with a cattle grid and beside the cattle grid was a hanging arm of signs. The Coachhouse, The Clocktower, The Lodge, Gamekeeper's Cottage, East and West Wings. The signs were slices of white wood, with the black letters neatly etched. 'The Wild,' William mused, and he set out to make a sign. He chose one of the Ashdown Forest logs and cut a sideways slice. He planed it smooth, pressing down on the soft wood with both his hands, and then with a chisel he carved 'The Wild' into the wood. The wood came away in tiny funnels and the pleasure it gave him was low down like a wave. He filled the whitened grooves with dark brown paint and when it was dry he varnished it, laying one silk coat over the next. The wood turned to a honey sheen and the bark stayed rough and frilled. He turned the small sign over and began varnishing the back, sweeping each stroke like a caress, and when he had finished he hung it with the rest.

The next day an envelope was pushed through the front door. It was delivered early before anyone was up. Mr William Strachan, Esquire, it said. There was no stamp. 'Someone's been working hard.' William flashed the letter round. Tess saw a long list of names scrawled down the middle of the page. 'They all object,' he said. 'But unfortunately the people who object the most are Major and Mrs Darlby who live next door.'

William stood up and looked out of the window. Just over the fence he could see the narrow garden, shaded by trees, where the retired couple from The Coachhouse were examining their lawn. The children all knelt up on their benches and peered out, while right beside the window William tore the letter up.

'What's Esquire?' Honour asked.

'Esquire,' William sat down in his chair, 'means a man of property. A man who owns land.' They looked at each other seriously. 'Very good question, Honour. Well done.'

That afternoon he let Sandy drive the van. He sat her on his knee and let her steer while he worked the pedals with his feet. They went right down to the big house and turned around in the gravel drive.

'Can I have a go?' Tess asked, leaning forward from the back. Sandy was steering up the hill again, her small hands under William's on the wheel as they headed for the cattle grid.

'Whoops!' William jerked the van as if to run right over the tree of signs and Sandy squealed and shrieked.

'Can I have a go?' Tess tried again, but William was shifting Sandy off his lap.

'Right, that's enough, only those with a driver's licence from now on,' and he drove on to the road.

They were visiting the family who ran the biodynamic farm. It was where the Strachans had stayed when they first came down from Scotland. 'Can't I go too?' Tess had asked, and William had shrugged and held open the back door of the van. William knew the Bremmers from another life, when they'd lived in a bungalow in Aberdeen. They'd had a television then and a freezer full of food – fish fingers, burgers, and vegetables in cubes. They'd eaten chocolate bars and sliced white bread, and hadn't even known that the skin of the potato was the most important part. But now almost everything they ate came from their land. They had six children, all large and creamy-skinned, and Tess watched the oldest boy for any signs. After all, he'd been born into that other life with KitKats and baked beans, the sugar from boxed cereal pumping round his heart, but as far as Tess could see he looked just the same.

Mrs Bremmer gave them parsnip soup with swirls of cream, and a slice of homemade bread. There was carrot salad with apple vinegar that got inside your nose and a sprinkling of sunflower seeds. Afterwards they ate white yoghurt with honey from the Bremmers' bees.

'So,' William told Martin Bremmer, 'Francine has taken both the rooms. You know Francine? Jake's mother from Class Six? We met at a parents' evening at the end of last term.'

Tess's spoon was clinking against the ceramic ridges of her bowl. 'My mother,' she said, looking up.

'Tess's mother,' William agreed. 'She's rented both the rooms.'

The Bremmers both turned to Tess and smiled.

There was a health-food shop in a cordoned-off section of the barn, where huge tin barrels were filled with oats, barley, raisins, hazelnuts, dried apricots, wheatgerm, millet, rice and flour. There were dried apple rings for treats. William ordered huge brown packets of everything they had, and the Bremmers' oldest boy helped load them into the van. William counted and re-counted the money. He laid down two separate sheaves of notes. 'This is Francine's share,' he said. 'If I could have separate change?'

Mrs Bremmer looked up. 'But you're planning to eat together?'

'Of course, of course.' Wiliam laughed. 'We've only got one kitchen.' He shook his head and smiled. 'Communal living, eh?' Then he noticed the children, all hovering by the door, and added, 'It's all working out quite well.'

Sandy and Doon shared a bedroom with bookshelves right across one wall. They had a dressing-up box spilling out with glitter, sequins, turbans and raw silk, and every night before they went to sleep William went in and sang to them. Tess could hear his voice drift down through the floorboards, accompanied by the low hum of his guitar.

'You can go in too,' Francine said, catching her listening at the bottom of the stairs.

'Are you sure?' Tess waited until, with Francine's

prompting, William asked her in himself. Tess curled up on the end of Doon's bed and let the warm songs seep into her skin.

'There was a fair maid who lived by the shore,
May the wind blow high or low.
No one could she find to comfort her mind,
She sang all alone on the shore.'

William's heavy hair hung low over his eyes and his arms cradled the guitar. Tess could have stayed listening for ever.

'There was a sea captain who sailed the salt sea,
May the wind blow high or low.
"I'll die, I'll die," the captain did cry,
"If I can't have that maid on the shore."'

Often the songs were tragic. Stories of mermaids, ship-wrecks, or Red Indians revenging themselves on newly settled whites. 'A happy one, Dad,' Doon begged. 'Please,' and William bent low over his guitar.

'Bottle of wine, fruit of the vine,
when you goin' to let me get sober.
Leave me alone and let me go home.
Won't you goin' let me start over.'

'Bottle of wine, fruit of the vine . . .' Tess sang to Jake and he slapped his hand down over the top bunk and told her to shut up.

'Why don't you like him?' she asked, and he looked at her with his clear serious face and said, 'He's after Mum.'

After supper, as the evenings started to get cold, William invited everyone to listen to his bedtime songs. He sat cross-legged on a cushion in the giant fireplace and Francine and the children crowded in around him. After several songs the person closest to the flames would start to roast and soon they'd crawl out over a throng of legs to swap with whoever was sitting in the draught from the back door. William sang a song about a woman. A woman with long black hair. She was fair with long black hair. But each time he sang the song something tripped him up. 'She was fair, with long ge – . . . b-black hair.' He stumbled and as the chords twanged and his fingers slipped, Francine blushed and Honour, Doon and Sandy laughed uncomfortably.

'What's ge . . . black?' Tess asked, as she helped Doon pick grass for her guinea-pig in the field behind the house. Doon smiled coldly and said the real words of the song were 'She was fair with long golden hair.' Doon had stopped picking and was squatting on her thin legs. She glanced up at Tess. 'He used to sing it for my Mummy,' she said. 'He didn't have to change the words for her.'

When Tess didn't answer, Doon added, 'She's the prettiest woman in the world. I've got a photo under my pillow.' But she said it quietly because William didn't like to hear anyone mention Felicity's name. At first Tess thought it was because she'd died. But after a while she realized it was because Felicity was evil. A sort of devil woman witch who'd tried to strangle him and draw out the last drop of his blood.

'He fought with all he had to get those girls,' Francine told a friend. 'After all, why should the woman get them automatically?' But as she talked she held tight on to Tess's arm. 'He was just as involved as her. More so even,' she said. 'Changing nappies, bathing them, and in the end she gave in and let them go.'

'He must have brought quite a case against her.'

'Oh he did,' she said. 'He most certainly did. It went through all the courts . . .' And sensing how hard Tess was listening she let her voice drift away.

Dear Dad,

One day Odin and Vili and Ve were striding along the frayed edges of the land where the earth meets the sea. They came across two fallen trees with their roots ripped out of the ground: one was an ash, the other an elm. Then the sons of Bor raised them and made from them the first man and woman. Odin breathed into them the spirit of life; Vili offered them sharp wits and feeling hearts; and

33

Ve gave them the gifts of hearing and sight. The man was called Ash and the woman Embla and they were given Midgard to live in. All the families and nations and races of men are descended from them.

I expect you knew that already.

Hope you're well. I'm very well. William is directing a school play. I'm not old enough to be in it, or even to see it.
Love Tess

William was proud to be Scottish, proud to have lived the first two years of his life in Cammothmore, but he liked to tell the story that an ancestor of his had travelled to America on the *Mayflower*, and somehow got hold of real Red Indian blood. When he told this story he turned to show his profile, which was crooked with a hard slug of a nose, and even though his hair was blond, his eyes were narrow and ink black. Francine laughed and told him to stop showing off, and Tess wondered how a man could be so handsome *and* cook ravioli *and* play the guitar. William's face and arms were dark brown from tackling the wild but the rest of his body was brilliant white.

'You're too pale to be a Red Indian,' Jake said, and William's eyes clouded over. 'Pale face,' Jake added as if he hadn't noticed, even though everyone else had quietened down. Jake folded his arms into the position of a chief and sang, 'Pow wow, Pow wow, in the name of the olden cow. We are the red men, feathers-in-our-head men, down upon the dead men. Pow wow.'

It was hard not to smile. Sandy slipped off her father's knee. 'Jake, sing it again,' she said, and for a moment they all chorused 'Pow wow, Pow wow,' copying Jake as he moved his hands in a quick rally of complicated movements, swooping down with 'dead men' and ending with a satisfying slap of flesh on the final low 'Pow wow'. 'We are the red men, feathers-in-our-head men, down upon the dead men. Pow wow.'

'Who'd like seconds?' Francine asked quickly before anyone could start again, and she reached down the table for William's plate.

For the first few months, William had cooked. He'd made lasagne, cheese fondue, cornmeal muffins and banana bread. But gradually it was left to Francine to make supper almost every night.

'This wasn't really the agreement,' Tess heard her say softly to him as she leant over the washing up, and William shook his head and smiled. 'You're so right, Francine,' he told her. 'We mustn't let things slide. It's not that you mind, I know, it's just the principle of the thing.' He promised that they'd cook on alternate nights whatever his work load, his marking, or the demands on his time now he'd volunteered to take on the school play. After all, Francine was now training to be a Kindergarten teacher and was out of the house all day.

A week later William drew up a rota. It was a calendar

of the month with small square boxes in different colours for each day. Sandy – lay table. Doon – sweep floor. Tess – dry up. Jake – wash up. Honour – help Francine to cook. The next day the entire rota changed. Tess – wash up. Doon – lay table, Sandy – sweep floor, Jake – help cook, Honour – dry up. On the weekend there were double tasks which lasted the whole month. Tess's was the downstairs bathroom. Every Sunday she was to clean the bathroom until the whole room shone. Jake's job was to tidy the back hall. Sort out the coats and the boots and shake the door mat. 'Sweep and wash the floor.' William went through the details of each job.

'Pathetic,' Jake said. 'In the time it took him to do the rota he could have cleaned the house himself.'

But what disturbed Tess were the colours. 'So you can find your chore with speed and accuracy,' William explained. Honour was purple. She looked beautiful dotted across the chart. Jake was red. Why couldn't she be red? Doon and Sandy were green and blue. But for Tess, out of the whole rainbow sheen of pencils from their box of Caran d'Ache, William had chosen brown.

William opened the larder and checked to see if they had HP Sauce. It was one of the luxuries he allowed himself. HP Sauce with shepherd's pie, hollandaise with broccoli, and he thought of Felicity and how she had once said they were the things that should never be apart.

'William?' The voice behind him was ready with a whine. 'William?'

'What is it?'

'I can't find Mum.'

'Well . . . have you looked in the garden?'

Tess was staring up at him, her pupils blackening her eyes. 'She's not there.'

William turned to peer into the larder. He could see silverfish slithering in the dim light, skating over the shelves, running up the sides of empty jars Francine was collecting to make jam. There was a smell in the larder of dried oatmeal and bran, a strange old-fashioned smell of self-sufficiency and good. He breathed in once more to strengthen his convictions and turned to Tess. 'I'm sorry, Tess,' he said, 'but I don't know where your Mummy is.' He smiled and pulled the HP Sauce from behind the store of black-eyed beans.

Tess wandered out into the garden. 'Mum.' She couldn't remember why she wanted her now but the longer she wasn't there the more she seemed to need her. 'MUUUMM!' She kicked her feet into the lawn, and then an upstairs window opened and Francine leant out. 'What is it?'

'Where were you?'

Francine looked down at Tess annoyed. 'Nowhere.'

But now Tess realized the window she had opened was in William's room.

'What is it?' Francine leant a little further out.

'Nothing. I can't find Jake.' Without looking up again Tess stamped off round the side of the house.

'Odin!' William's voice was stern. 'Odin, bad bad cat!' Tess could hear him, trembling on the edges of control. 'Drop it, Odin, drop it.'

Tess ran back towards the kitchen. 'It's all right,' she called, but like thick whiskers sticking out from Odin's face she saw the wings, the legs, the yellow beak of a bird. Odin was growling at William through the bird's body, and William was ordering him to let it go. As soon as he saw Tess, Odin dropped the bird at her feet. 'Bad cat,' William said again, and the bird gave one last quiver. Odin curled around Tess's legs, shimmying his tail back and forth, willing her to defy William and run her fingers flat against his head.

'You'd better get Jake and bury that poor creature at the bottom of the garden.'

'All right,' said Tess, and before William went inside he turned and shook his head at her, as if deeply disappointed by the whole affair. 'Do a good job now,' he said.

The bird was a starling with one broken, hanging wing, its eyes newly clouded over. Odin went with them to dig the grave. He didn't look repentant. He kept his tail straight up and quivering, and while Jake squatted down to dig the hole he let his body fall sideways, flat against Jake's back. 'You like it here, don't you?' Tess nuzzled his warm fur, and Odin smiled with his orange eyes, his nose a velvet slope of pink. 'Naughty cat,' she muttered then, in case anyone could overhear, and Jake, raking the earth flat, stuck a stick into the ground to mark the spot.

'When we get our chickens,' William said that night at supper, 'we'll have to watch out for Jake's cat.'

Jake laughed. 'It's nature,' he said. 'And nature is cruel.'

'Perhaps there's a different pet you'd like to have?' William asked, but the only animals Jake liked were wild. 'I wouldn't mind a lama,' he said, 'or a wolf.' And afterwards he sneered, 'That shut him up.'

William's new van was rusty round the edges, and the walls above the wheels were lacy thin. He towed it home behind the old one, with Mr Jenkinshaw rattling at the wheel. Mr Jenkinshaw had on an old man's hat, its checked peak low down in an arc over his face, so that behind the windscreen of the high blue van it was just possible to forget about his nose.

'I don't understand.' Francine stood beside the half-built garage, watching as they manoeuvred the van in. 'Now you've got two vans, except this one's even more decrepit than the old one.'

'I'll use it for spare parts,' William said, and with Mr Jenkinshaw's help he parked it as far as it would go against their neighbour's wall.

William let the children decorate the van. He brought out the ends of all the pots of paint and suggested they paint rainbows right over the roof, but Jake wanted to paint a duck-billed platypus and Sandy had already started with a flower. She dipped her brush in yellow and made a splodge over the handle of the door.

'They don't make these vans any more.' William stroked the bonnet, and Tess leant against the van's blue side. She understood now why William had hooted, frantic and delighted, when once they'd passed another identical van on the road. 'Wave, everyone, wave!' he'd told them, and his three daughters had shrieked up to the front.

'I don't know what to paint.' Doon was staring, miserable, her thin arms hanging hopeless at her sides.

'Shall we paint the wheels?' Tess knelt down beside her and together they swirled their brushes, orange and red, into the metal swoop of grey. The paint lapped up on to the tyres, splashed out over the drive, dribbling molten colours along the insides of their arms. They were so crouched and busy, moving from wheel to wheel, that they didn't notice when the Newlands, who owned the flat in the East Wing, slowed to watch them, the windows of their estate car tightly shut.

'What are you doing?' William startled them. 'Not the wheels, you silly girls! What if I need one for a spare?'

His face was closed and angry and he pulled the brushes out of their hands. 'Of all the things – ' he shook his head and threw the brushes into a bowl.

Doon looked at Tess. 'Stupid,' she said and she went to stand with her own sisters on the other side of the van.

'Good morning, Class Four.' Mr Paul stood behind his desk and lead them in the morning prayer.

'I look into the world
Wherein there shines the sun
Wherein there lie the stones
Wherein there shine the stars
The plants they live and grow
The beasts they feel and live . . .'

They did their exercises. Jumping sideways as they raised their arms. Stretching their fingers and bouncing on the balls of their feet.

'Now,' Mr Paul said when they'd settled in their seats, 'let me tell you about the beginning of all that has ever happened, all that is remembered or forgotten in the world.'

As Tess dug in her garden she told herself this story. How Asgard was a mighty stronghold, a place of green plains and shining palaces, where Odin, Allfather, the oldest and greatest of the gods once lived. Tess knelt over her store of winter bulbs. She was going to map out her territory with crocuses, and the centre-piece would be a bright-blue rose. She'd seen a picture of these roses in East Grinstead market, unlikely flowers the colour of summer sky, and she'd talked on and on about them until Francine had bought one for her, secretly, so that in the spring William would be amazed when it unfurled.

'Tess!' Jake was calling her. As he got nearer he lowered his voice. 'Do you want to come?'

'Where?'

Jake looked at her as if she were an idiot. 'Down to the phone box.' He opened his eyes wide to show just what he meant.

Tess stabbed a long hole with the dibber, dropped in a bulb and packed it in with earth.

'Come on!' Jake leant down and took hold of her arm.

'Wait one minute.' Tess scrabbled all her bulbs back into their paper bag.

'Hurry, or we'll be late,' Jake said, and pulling her with him he ran round the side of the house, through the back gate and out on to the road. The estate of Laurel Hill was part of a hilltop hamlet. There was one pub, one shop, and running through the hamlet, past the church, a winding road that brought a bus at eleven minutes before or after each alternate hour. At the bottom of the hill there was a red-ridged phone box.

'Quick!' Jake let go of Tess and ran, his arms outstretched, his feet leaping and skeltering a second behind his legs. Tess gripped her bag of bulbs. The hill was so steep she had to stop herself from taking off into the air, her plimsolled feet grappling for contact as she tried to slow herself with straight jolts of her knees. 'It's ringing!' Jake called, and his speed picked up. It was as if the whole red box was ringing. The noise burst through each pane of glass, desperate, calling, urging them on. Jake was running too fast to stop. He had to use the arm of the wooden bench beside the phone box to catch himself, and he hung on to it, waiting for his feet to slow and wheel around. But by now Tess had caught up with him and she was pulling at the door, slipping her fingers into the tiny handle and using all her weight to ease the hinge. They squeezed inside together and fought over the phone.

'Yes? Hello?' It was their father's flat anonymous code. 'Hello? Hello?'

Jake wrenched the receiver to his ear. 'Dad?' The voice at the other end lightened as a real person, fresh out of disguise, jumped through. Tess leant against the glass and waited. Jake had the phone pressed so close to his hot face it was hardly worth the effort to try and overhear. 'Yes,' he breathed, 'uh-huh,' and she couldn't imagine what there was to say.

'You could come for the Christmas Fair,' Jake suggested. 'I mean, it's pretty stupid, but you might think it's quite funny . . . or . . . maybe . . . maybe we could come up? Visit you in London?'

It was warm against the phone-box wall, the soft ridges, peeling paint were heated with late-autumn sun, fuelling up the box with an old grey metal smell of ash.

Jake listened. 'Yes,' he muttered then. Tess could tell he wasn't pleased. 'Yes. Yup. All right, here's Tess.' He passed her the phone.

'Hello, Dad?' She'd forgotten for a moment that she'd have to talk. 'Yes, I'm fine.' Without waiting to think she told him about her garden and how William had marked out five separate plots. 'If Jake doesn't want his I'm going to have it and make it part of mine.' She told him about the blue rose, the packet it was wrapped in, and how they wouldn't know which colours the crocuses were until next spring. 'Dad? Dad are you all right?' He'd started to cough and while he coughed she heard him rustle through some papers on his desk. 'I'm knitting socks,' she added quickly, hoping to keep his interest up. They're for William's birthday, and the funniest thing of all,' she had to let him know, 'is that his birthday is on the same day as yours!'

'Really?' There was a short silence and then he asked to say goodbye to Jake.

'Might you?' Jake's whole face had brightened up. 'The Christmas Fair?' He promised to pass the message on to Mum.

They walked back up the hill. 'I wish we had a phone,' Jake said. 'But Pale Face is too mean.'

'He's not mean,' Tess said, and they trudged on in silence.

That night Tess woke up in a damp cold dip of sheet. Her nightdress had rolled up around her waist but the fringes of it were still wet. For a while she lay still, her heart heavy, her eyes closed. Eventually she rolled out of bed. She pulled off the sheet, screwed it into a ball and pushed it under the bed. Just before school tomorrow she'd bury it among the dirty clothes, and then Francine, when she rifled through the laundry, would understand.

Sandy was her greatest fear. 'Ugh, someone's pissed in the dirty clothes. Yuk, Yuk, Yuk.' She'd turned, her eyes narrow, striking white ash into Tess's heart. 'Maybe it was that stinky Odin cat?'

Tess had shrunk into her seat. 'It was not!' But as soon as breakfast was over she had gone and pushed the sheet into the machine herself.

Now Tess peeled off her nightie and tiptoed towards her mother's door. She opened it a crack and saw Francine's long, warm body, rising just a fraction with each breath. She had the striped blanket she liked to spread over each new bed pulled halfway up her arms, and in the half-light the raised flowers of her nightdress shimmered in the air. Tess stood there shivering, her body pale and damp, and trying not to breathe she slithered up on to the high bed. She was careful, careful not to wake Francine as she inched herself under the sheets, easing the blanket over, and tucking in against her mother's back. Tess took a long slow breath. The smell of her, the dry, familiar, secret smell, began to warm her, and soon the silky sheen of cotton and the tickling of her long dark hair lulled her towards sleep.

Tess only ever peed once during a night. Once was bad enough but at least it meant that after it was over she could sink in safety into a luxurious sleep. It was her secret and even Jake wasn't allowed to know. He mustn't know, and the most important thing was that Honour, Doon and Sandy never find out. William . . . it made Tess shrink to think of it . . . and she promised herself that William would never have to know because after tonight she'd stop. Tess curled closer in to her mother and thought of the weeks, the long safe stretches where everything stayed dry. 'It's over now, isn't it?' she'd say hopefully and Francine would stroke her hair. 'We always knew you'd grow out of it, didn't we?' It was the only safe time to say it. When it was over. And then, a few days later, there was the awful inevitable evidence that it was not.

★

'Mum?' Tess asked the next morning. 'Did Jake tell you about the Christmas Fair?'

'Mmmm.'

'About Dad? He said to tell you that he was going to come?'

'Really?' Francine had a dreamy morning look.

'He is,' Tess insisted. 'He said he was. He asked Jake to tell you.'

'OK.' Francine slipped off her nightdress, the static lifting her hair as she turned away to dress. Her back was freckled in an arc across each shoulder and as she bent down her hair swung forward until it nearly touched her toes. Tess could see the muscles in her legs, lengthening as she swooped down, scooping for her pale wool tights, and the way the two halves of her bottom divided in a line. It was cold this morning and Francine hurried as she slipped on a long-sleeved vest, the two creamy shades meeting in the middle, almost touching, almost hiding the deep eye of her navel. Tess sat wrapped in her mother's blanket, and thought how beautiful she looked. Like a ballerina or a cartwheeling princess. If she looked like that herself, she'd go to school without a dress. She wondered if everyone who'd ever seen Francine realized she was far more beautiful than William's old wife.

'Come on, lazy bones.' Francine pulled trousers on over her tights. 'You can't lie around all day.'

And Tess ran, naked, her flesh stinging into bumps, all raised up and reddened where the pee had scoured her legs. 'Jake,' she called as she scrambled for some clothes. 'Time to get up.' She saw the shine of his dark head burrow down under the sheet.

Doon's guinea-pig lived in a cage at the bottom of her bed, and every evening before supper Doon picked grass for it in the field behind the house. William had made a run for it outside and there were oblong marks across the lawn where, on mild afternoons, Lupin was put out to graze. Lupin was out there now, his feet hidden by the long hair of his coat, his flat nose snuffling for food. As Tess watched she saw Odin slip round the corner of the house. He trailed his body close along the ground and slunk up to the mesh, his ears were back, his tail was low, and then with one swift movement he swiped his paw to lift the corner of the run. Lupin's stout body froze.

'Odin!' Tess pounced. 'You naughty cat!' She bundled him, his legs straight out, his teeth half bared, up into her arms and carried him back to the house. She threw him down on to her bed. 'You've got to be kind to other creatures.' Tess lay down beside him and let him curl into the space above her knees. She stroked his paws, pressing gently on each pad to force out a claw, and she curled his tail for him right round to the tip of his nose. He purred luxuriously, showing one fang occasionally for pride, but as long as Tess refrained from turning back his ears to see the little lanes of pink, she knew he didn't mind. Odin was a perfect tabby, thick with tiger stripes. 'King of the Cats,' Jake called him, and lulled by his deep purr Tess fell asleep.

'Tess!' It was Sandy, sent to wake her up. 'It's your turn to lay the table.' She slammed the door as she went out so that Odin leapt up and scooted for safety to the top bunk, catching Tess's leg with a sharpened claw and tearing at the flesh.

'Ow!' Tess pressed down hard on it to stop the blood and, hobbling for sympathy, she made her way through to find the knives and forks.

William was cutting stems of holly, and looking for a perfect arc of fir. It was the first day of Advent and he planned to make a wreath. He needed a branch so soft and pliant that he could tuck one end into its tail. 'Gather round,' he called to his girls, and Tess appeared from nowhere, jumping down from the branches of a tree.

'What, William? What?' she said, all hot and breathless, and it made him feel foolish somehow to be stopped short like this before he'd even planned what he was going to say.

He looked coldly at her and leant up to pull a branch down over his head. 'It's long enough, and young and supple,' he said, 'and it will bend round to make our wreath. Has it got plenty of needles, nice and thick? It has.' He took out his knife and spliced it in a clear clean sideways cut.

His daughters nodded, scuffling dry leaves with their toes, and followed him obediently back into the house.

'Can I wind the red ribbon?' Tess wanted to know, and he held the wreath while she bound it round with satin. Her hands were small and square and clumsy, her nails dirtier than Sandy's ever were.

'That's enough.' He had to shake her free, and he gave Honour the job of attaching the four candles. He made a pulley from the remaining ribbon and hung it from a hook above the fire. 'Tonight we'll light the first candle.' He wasn't saying who'd be chosen for this task. The youngest, the oldest? The child whose initial was closest to A? He smiled and pulled the wreath high into the air.

For William's socks Tess had chosen red and blue. With socks you started at the top, and so the legs were stripy and the heels and toes, when Tess eventually got to them, would stand out red. She wanted them to come up to the knee and taper in over the ankle, but what she hadn't anticipated was the length of William's feet. It was possible she'd run out of wool before the second instep and Miss Tindal, the handwork teacher, would have to find her more.

The handwork room at school was full of wool. Wool

and felt and fleeces, spinning wheels and embroidery thread, and Miss Tindal's fingers were all torn and worn from sorting through the stock. Tess imagined her spinning late at night, the fuzz of wool dragging at her skin, and she wondered if one day her own hands would turn raw. Tess was the first in her class to move on to socks. The others were one step behind, still stuffing animals, but her multi-coloured cockerel was already perched above Francine's bed, its plumage strips of felt, its pipe cleaner feet wound round and round with thread.

When they'd first started with Miss Tindal she'd showed them how to make knitting needles out of wood. They'd rounded the sides, sharpened the ends, and sanded them smooth so they didn't catch the wool. When everyone was ready she laid out a sheep's fleece. The greasy, waterproof smell of it stung inside your nose and it hung together like a coat. Miss Tindal showed them how to card the wool, lightening it, sorting it, turning it to fluff, and when it was feather light and see-through they spun it into wool. It took a whole year of preparation before they were ready for a stitch.

Since then Tess had knitted a flannel, crocheted a table-mat, sewn a felt animal, and now she'd come back to knitting. But this time she was allowed plastic needles with numbers on the ends, and any coloured wool.

'What is that disgusting stripy rag?'

'Nothing.' Tess narrowed her eyes at Jake, but she hid her knitting under a cushion when William joined them in the fireplace for songs.

'Let's sing "While shepherds washed their socks,"' Sandy giggled, and Honour brought out her *Oxford Book of Carols*. William started in his rich, encouraging voice.

'While shepherds watched their flocks by night,
All seated on the ground,
The angel of the Lord came down
And glory shone around.'

It was hard not to join in.

'Fear not, said he, for mighty dread
Had seized their troubled minds,
Glad tidings of great joy I bring
To you and all mankind.'

The fire flared up and Doon had to slide out and swap places with Francine. William's voice was low and deep and he gave each carol the occasional strum on his guitar. 'Silent night, holy night, all is calm, all is bright.' Tess had never heard anything so beautiful.

In a pause, while Francine crawled out into the welcome draught, Jake cleared his throat.

'When Jesus Christ was yet a child
He had a garden fair and wild'

He'd chosen the last carol in the book. It was low, and
mournful.

'Wherein he cherished roses fair
And wove them into garlands there.'

Jake's voice drooped down with a hint of menace at the
end of every line. Honour joined in on the second verse,
her voice quivering and beautiful, and for the first time a
smile flickered between them.

'Now once as summer time drew nigh,
There came a group of children by,
And seeing roses on the tree,
With shouts they plucked them merrily.

Do you bind roses in your hair?
They cried in scorn to Jesus there.
The boy said humbly "Take I pray
All but the naked thorns away."'

Jake's smile turned into a grin and his voice swooped
down into an abyss.

'Then of the thorns they made a crown,
And with rough fingers pressed it down,
Till on his forehead fair and young
Red drops of blood like roses sprung.'

Sandy's eyes were bright and glittering. 'Red drops of blood.' She pressed her hands to her head. 'Ow, Daddy, it hurts.'

William hauled her on to his lap. 'Jake, there are little ones here.' Then he remembered Honour. 'That was an inappropriate choice,' he said to her, and he clapped shut his book.

Mr Paul stood under the Class Four Advent wreath. 'Listen,' he said. 'Who can hear the sound of grass growing? Who needs less sleep than a bird? Who is so eagle-eyed that, by day and by night, he can see the least movement a hundred leagues away?'

'Loki?' Tess suggested.

'Heimdall and Heimdall and Heimdall,' said Mr Paul.

Mr Paul told them how Heimdall visited Ai and Edda, great-grandfather and great-grandmother, and how he won the best position by the fire, ate the tastiest bits of the supper and got the best position in the middle of the bed.

Nine months after his visit, Edda gave birth to a son. From the first his skin was wrinkled, his hands were chapped, his fingers all stubby and his knuckles were knotted. His back was twisted and his feet too large. Ai and Edda called him Thrall.

When Thrall was a young man he met a girl. She was bow-legged, the soles of her feet were damp and discoloured, her sunburned arms were peeling and she had the squashed nose of a boxer. Her name was Thir the Drudge. They had a cluster of contented children. The names of their sons were Cattle Man and Coarse, Shouter and Horse-Fly, Concubine Keeper and Stinking, Clot, Gross, the sluggard Drott, and Legjaldi, whose legs were as thick as tree trunks. Thrall and Thir also had daughters. There were Oaf and BlobNose, Dumpy and Hefty-Thighs, Noisy and Servant, Peg of Oak, Bundle of Rags, and bony Tronubeina, who had legs as long and skinny as a crane. These were the offspring of Ai and Edda and from these children stem the race of thralls.

William was late home now almost every night. He'd decided to direct his own version of *Oedipus*, and the whole project was going to take the rest of the school year.

'We'll give the play a modern slant,' he said. 'Man railing against discipline, the ties that bind. Fate. Why shouldn't we marry who we want?' He raised his eyebrows at Francine. 'What was that?' he asked, cupping his good ear. But he still didn't hear when she asked him if he wanted grated cheese. 'I've found an actress to play Oedipus's wife. She's not exactly an older woman, that would be too hard, but she's got a special quality. Light, translucent almost.'

Jake put down his fork. 'Not that spotty girl with the long hair? Albino Al?'

'Alison?' William darted round.

'She's a freak,' Jake smiled. 'Everyone thinks so.'

'Well I don't.' But William's face fell into a frown.

'Will we be allowed to see it?' Tess asked.

'No.' William forked up a mouthful and looked round with irritation. 'Is there no cheese?'

'It's only for the Upper School,' Honour said.

'Maybe I could watch rehearsals.' Tess knelt up on the bench.

William was eating now. Eating and thinking, a thick frown ridging across his head.

'Maybe I – '

'Shhh Tess, not now,' Francine said, and she walked round the table and sprinkled cheese on to William's plate herself.

On the morning of the Christmas Fair Victor parked his long sleek car in front of William's van. He leant across to open the door for Georgina and she slipped out into the mud. She had on pale shoes and her coat came almost to the ground. She pulled it tight around her and followed Victor up the ramp which William had lined with planks.

Tess watched them from the far end of the garden.

'Dad!' It was Jake, shouting to them from the front door, and he sped out and stood awkwardly, smiling, his head bobbing about with joy.

'Tess was right,' Tess heard her father say. 'It is rather an extraordinary place.' He looked towards the neat mounds of onions and potatoes, the frosted garden raked over and waiting for the spring.

Georgina glanced dispassionately around. 'Yes,' she added, 'a real homestead.' And they all three began to laugh.

'Odin,' Jake called. He wanted Victor to see Odin, to see how fierce he was and strong. Tess could see Odin watching them from the garage scaffolding, curled against a pole, and when Jake went on calling him, he unwound himself and jumped with a lazy thud on to the ground.

'He doesn't look too impressed with us,' Georgina laughed, and it was true, Odin was circling them haughtily, sneering almost, with half-closed eyes.

'Be good,' Jake warned him, 'and I'll see if I can find you something at the Christmas Fair.' He tried to stroke him as he sauntered off.

Jake and Tess sat in the slippery beige back of their father's car. They slid over the cattle grid close behind William's van, which shuddered and backfired as it struggled out. They followed dutifully, watching the silhouettes of the three girls hover between Francine's and William's seats, and then with a swerve and a rush of speed they pulled out past them and were away, speeding sickeningly along the country road.

'Lost them,' Jake grinned, but Tess thought she'd caught the edge of a slow sulk in William's jaw as he'd tried to push his van on to a higher speed.

The school hall had been transformed into a fair. There were stalls of stuffed animals, plaited loaves of bread, corn dollies tied with ribbons, and Christmas decorations made from wood. There were framed paintings, the corners rounded off, of men and women, cowering in a kind of glow. The frames were chiselled, dented with millions of marks, and in the dip of each hollow you could see the natural pattern of the wood.

Mr Paul was standing by the cake stall eyeing the different shapes of cake. Tess bustled through the crowd to get to him. 'Mr Paul?' But she had to wait while he passed money over for a walnut loaf, and when she turned back to point her father out to him the others had all drifted off. 'Dad?' She tried to push back through the crowd. 'Jake?' But she couldn't see them above the sea of heads.

Tess looked into the gym, where a woodwork exhibition was on display, and peered through the window of the music room, where parents sat obediently as the Lower

School orchestra drilled thunderously away. Her own classroom had been turned into a candle-dipping room and she found her mother holding on to a long tallow wick, her hair just skimming the hot vat of wax.

'Mum!' Tess ran in to her. But the woman who ran the school shop was talking, telling Francine she wouldn't be needing their charitable contribution to school fees now that Tess and Jake could be put down as teachers' children and get their education free.

'No, no!' Francine blushed and her candle hung there, waiting for its dip. 'Tess and Jake haven't suddenly become teachers' children. William Strachan has just rented us some rooms, that's all. I mean obviously . . . well . . .' – she reached for Tess's hand – 'Obviously if there is any change . . .'

'I see.' The woman nodded, and Francine, pale now, bent low over the wax.

Tess chose a wick and dipped it into the vat. She let it hang there for a minute before she pulled it up. She could mould a beeswax candle for her father to make up to him for not getting any socks. 'It's not working.' She squinted at the first thin film, and Francine told her she had to keep dipping, on and on, until the candle was thick enough to stand. There were three vats in the room and Tess hurried between them, dipping her candle, watching the filmy layers, transparent, cloud over and turn yellow as slowly, slowly they built up. The room was warm and cloying, her own class's Norse Myth paintings covering the walls.

She bit her lip impatiently as she swung her candle, waiting for each layer to dry.

Outside the sky was growing dark. People passed by in little groups, rushing and laughing, showing off the things they'd bought. Tess wanted to abandon her candle, leave it to melt back into liquid wax, but now she'd decided to give it to her father she had to wait until the end. Eventually it was thick enough to stand, just, if you melted it quite solidly against a saucer, and the lady wrapped it up for her. 'Thanks,' Tess said, and ran as fast as she could along the corridor and out through the main doors. Lights had been switched on in every room of the school, illuminating the paper-tissue friezes each class had made to decorate their rooms. Mr Paul had made Class Four a shepherds scene that stretched across two windows, with sheep and dogs, and a fire where orange flames danced between the wood.

Tess took great swallows of cold air. There was hardly anyone about, and then she saw Doon standing on her own, watching three girls skip inside a rope. Her pigtails stood out from her head, and her tights had wrinkled at the knee. 'Have you seen Jake?' Tess asked her, and without taking her eyes off the skipping Doon said he and Victor and Georgina were in the Long Room having tea.

At first Tess couldn't see them, pressed into the corner,

leaning towards each other over their plates. 'Jake,' she called, when she caught sight of his dark head, and she squeezed between the chairs. Jake hadn't heard her. He was eating cake and laughing. Laughing so hard crumbs flew out of his mouth. Even Georgina was laughing and Victor's shoulders shook. Tess slipped into a spare chair. She wanted to start laughing too, but she couldn't think what about. Instead she passed Victor the candle. 'I made it myself,' she said as he unwrapped it, and she watched his face as for a second he wondered what it was.

'Thank you.' He rolled it under his nose like a cigar.

'How marvellous.' Georgina reached for it, and she closed her eyes as she breathed in its honey smell.

'Where were you?' Jake glared at her, and when she didn't answer he kicked her under the table before passing over the last crumbs of his cake.

William's van was waiting, parked in the emptying field beside their father's dark-blue car. Jake and Tess shuffled forward to say goodbye to their father and as they did so, as they reached up for a kiss, Victor crumpled a note into each of their hands. 'For Christmas shopping,' he whispered, and Tess felt how her money was soft and worn. Even through the fingers of her fist she could smell its papery smell of smoke and leather. Georgina pulled her coat around her and nodded towards Francine. She didn't move or speak, but simply dropped her chin for a goodbye.

Tess and Jake were still clambering into the back of the van, pulling themselves up on to the metal floor, as the long car backed up, turned, and sped off out of the school gates. As Victor swung on to the main road he flashed his headlights pale gold, and for a moment everything was thrown into relief, the fence, the field, the startled cows, and the nobbled branches of the trees.

William turned his key sharply in the ignition, which clattered shrilly and then died. Tess saw his shoulders stiffen, her mother glance tenderly at him, and then with extra choke he charged the engine into life. Sandy and Doon, examining their purchases, were thrown towards each other in the back. 'Ow, get off,' they roared, and Honour, reading by the light of a tiny torch, told them to shut up. Jake was folding and re-folding his note. Tess could see the '10' from where she perched on the soft edge of the spare tyre, and she fingered hers in the pocket of her coat and tried to feel the sum like Braille.

'I feel quite strongly about this.' It was William's turn to dry the dishes and he stood with Francine in the sudden quiet of the house. 'Victor really shouldn't just hand out money without consulting us first.'

'Us?' Francine frowned, but really she looked pleased.

'It just doesn't seem fair. The children should be treated the same.'

Francine rubbed the inside of a cup and rinsed it under the tap.

'Yes,' she said, although she wasn't sure.

'I mean, Felicity doesn't turn up here and hand out great wads of cash.'

'William . . .' Francine started to laugh. It occurred to her that they were having their first row. 'You're being – ' But he cut her off by flinging down his tea towel and striding out of the room. Francine stood at the sink. The laughter that had bubbled up inside her was still there. She stooped to pick up the cloth and, ignoring the strict system of the rota, she wiped dry William's knives.

Jake was leaning over his bunk, his mouth and eyes pulling ghostlike upside down. 'Can you believe what William said to Dad?'

'What?'

'He asked Dad to take us off his hands for Christmas. Said he wanted to make a go of things with his wife.'

'Whose wife?'

'William's. He thinks Christmas might be just the time to patch things up.'

'Where would Dad take us?'

'Nowhere, you idiot. He doesn't celebrate Christmas. You know that.'

'Oh.' Tess rolled towards the wall to get away from him. She held her body tight. 'How do you know, anyway?'

'Dad told me. He told me in the Long Room when we were having tea.'

Tess closed her eyes, but behind them she was jumping, jumping from one narrow ledge to the next as cracks across a plateau opened up. The cracks got wider, turning into chasms until she was leaping and leaping for her life.

'He's a creep,' she heard Jake say. 'Dad thinks so as well. Dad does, and so do I.'

Jake was the only one who couldn't see the point of getting up. He yawned luxuriously and snuggled close into the poster jaws of a huge grizzly bear. It was the morning of William's birthday and Tess was sitting up in bed, feverishly knitting the last diminishing rows. This second sock was very slightly shorter than the first and occasionally she stopped and gave it a quick tug. Eventually the stitches of the toe were down to six, four, two, and then with one final loop the sock was closed and tightened with a knot. She bit the wool off bluntly with her teeth.

'Mum!' She raced to find the Sellotape, and there on the stairs were Doon and Sandy singing Happy Birthday with Honour accompanying them on her violin.

'He's coming downstairs!' Tess screamed and she rushed off to take her place as his daughters all began to Hip Hip Hooray him into his seat.

Francine had arranged holly in a spiky wreath around his bowl, and she'd made a special breakfast, muesli with apples finely grated in a curl over the top. There were small handfuls of oatmeal, barley, raisins and wheatgerm, sprinkled with nuts.

'Well, thank you.' William slid on to his chair, and Tess saw his eyes flick, counting up the cards. She wriggled with anticipation. There was no doubt her present had to be the best. William reached out and pulled the first bright package towards him and everyone held their breath.

'Morning,' Jake said, stumbling through the door, and he took his seat as if it were just any old morning of the year. 'What's this?' He flicked at the apple already browning on his plate, and Francine said 'Shhh!'

'Now, I wonder who this could be from?' William beamed, holding up a lumpen round of scratchy wrapping, and Sandy put her hand over her mouth and began to squeak. 'It feels very precious,' he said, weighing it solemnly in his hand, and carefully he stripped back the paper to reveal a bird's nest, all old and mouldy from the ground.

'Sandy.' He leant sideways and kissed her high forehead where chickenpox had left one small scar crescent like the moon. 'Thank you.' Tess could see he was genuinely touched.

'I found it on my own.'

'Did you now?' He reached for the next present. It was wrapped neatly, a rectangle, four corners sharp. 'I wonder what this could be?' Everybody laughed. 'It's from Francine,' he mused, turning it over as if he couldn't possibly imagine what it might be.

'It's a book!' Tess yelled. It was out before she could stop herself and everybody's laughter died away. 'I mean . . . it might not be . . .'

William frowned in concentration as he unwrapped it. 'The poetry of Robert Burns.' He gave Francine an understanding smile. 'Thank you, I shall enjoy owning this again.' He touched it for a moment to his heart.

Honour had embroidered him a picture. It was old-fashioned like a sampler with cross-stitch at the edge and in the middle was a tiny outline of a house. Beside the house a man stood with three children linked to each other at the palm, growing very slightly smaller like ducks along a pond. 'The proportions aren't quite right,' Honour craned to see, and she showed him how the man had come out bigger than the house.

'It's absolutely perfect,' he told her. 'A work of art.' He laid it across his plate with great appreciation.

'So now what do we have here?' The roll of the next present flopped across his hand. 'It feels like a tie,' he laughed, 'or a pair of socks.' He chuckled as if this was the least likely thing in the world that it could be. Tess gulped, shivery with waiting, and saw the small worms of the apple darkening brown. And then there they were, her socks unfurling out of the paper, still warm from knitting, a mound of lumpy wool.

William held one up by the toe. 'They look . . . very practical.' Tess wanted to tell him, in case he hadn't noticed, that she'd knitted every stitch of them herself.

'Thank you. Right.' He was moving on, glancing at his watch. A bookmarker from Doon and a small World Wildlife diary from Jake. 'Jake, what can I say?' William looked ridiculously pleased. 'That's wonderful.' He let his fingers trail through the diary, stroking each page as if Jake had pledged him the whole of the next year.

'Now eat up everyone,' he said, 'or we'll all be late for school.'

Tess tried one last time. 'Do you think you'll ever wear the socks?'

William paused, his mouth full, as if he might not recall what socks she meant. 'Oh, yes,' he nodded, chewing. 'Yes, I'm sure I'll find some opportunity for wearing them, maybe on that trip up Everest I've planned.' And he looked around the table to raise the volume of everybody's laugh.

'I've got some news about Christmas,' Francine said. 'We're going to stay with Liza.' She looked bright and cheerful as if this was going to be a real treat.

'Who's Liza?' Tess and Jake both stared.

'You don't remember Liza? Liza and Sam?' She faltered slightly. 'They've got a little girl now, Libby, who's three. I've been wanting to visit . . . Anyway, they've invited us for Christmas. Isn't that nice?'

'Is it?' Jake asked.

'I thought we were going to have Christmas here.' Tess pictured the giant tree William had brought home. It was so tall he'd had to leave the back doors of the van open to let the tip stick out over the road.

'It's very complicated.' Francine sighed. 'But William thinks . . . William wants . . . Well, children need their mothers. Especially at Christmas. So Felicity is going to come here for a few days.'

'I thought so,' Jake said.

'Felicity!' Tess was amazed.

'I'd like to see that.' Jake's eyes danced about.

'Well, you won't,' Francine said irritably. 'William wants us gone by Christmas Eve.' She walked into her room and very firmly shut the door.

But Felicity arrived before they'd had a chance to leave. She stepped out of an Escort, the driver leaping out to help her with her bags, and as she glided up the ramp beside the half-built garage, Tess saw she had a milky beauty, a floating golden beauty that had even the taxi driver trembling on his toes.

Tess, Doon and Sandy were playing badminton, the shuttlecock drifting about in the damp and gusty air. 'It's Mummy!' Sandy gasped, and dropping her racquet she ran to her and butted her body like a goat. 'Mummy!' Doon wailed and tears sprang from her eyes.

Tess trailed behind them as the taxi driver carried Felicity's bags into the house. 'Dad!' Doon called. 'Look, look!'

'William!' Tess shouted. She wanted to be the one to bring him the good news. 'She's here!' But William's face when he saw his wife was terrible. Something like a shock bulged out his eyes, and his forehead doubled and raised the low line of his hair. Tess opened her mouth to laugh, but then she saw Felicity look down at the soft folds of her coat. 'I know I should have told you . . .' she smiled. 'Pete and I . . .' She raised her hand to touch her stomach, which was pressing high against her shirt. She didn't seem to know that she had Doon's hand in hers because she pulled it with her, straining it to touch the baby's heart.

William stared at his feet. His face had darkened, the muscles in his cheeks working too hard. 'Yes,' he said, correcting like a teacher. 'You should have let us know.' He slammed a sheaf of cutlery down into the sink. The metal crashed and chimed and the noise of it brought the other children running, in time to see him stride out of the room.

'Dramatic as ever,' Felicity smiled, her lips pursed, and she knelt down to embrace her daughters, trying to take all three of them into her arms.

'Stop staring.' Jake kicked Tess and he pulled her through to their room where Francine was packing, hurriedly throwing clothes into a bag while outside the window William walked round and round the slushy lawn.

The afternoon was misty, pale, as if the sun might still come up, and Francine kept blinking as her hands gripped white against the wheel. 'Can't we go a bit faster?' Jake moaned, but Tess was with the car, watching the road, gulping with the effort to forestall a crash. The Ford Anglia they'd borrowed felt small and shaky after the backfiring bulk of William's van, and Tess wished that she could curl up and only wake once they were there.

'When will we arrive?' They'd cranked their way through Twelve Ashes and were safely heading out along the East Grinstead Road.

'Well, we head towards London and then . . . Oh God . . .' A lorry hurtled past. 'Then it's really quite some way from there.'

'Will we have to stop?'

'Yes, yes.' If she'd been able to spare the extra effort Francine would have asked them both to quieten down.

'Can we stop now?'

There was no answer. Tess could tell from the freckled side of Francine's face that there was nothing she would have liked more, but instead she peered into her mirror and grimaced at the line of cars building up behind her. 'You'll just have to wait.' Francine cranked up a gear, and as the engine rocked and whined someone behind them beeped.

Tess read to them from her mainlesson book. 'Not content with his faithful wife, Loki took off for Jotunheim to spend days and nights with Angrboda.' She'd written the whole story out in different shades of Caran d'Ache. 'Loki and Angrboda had three monstrous offspring. The eldest was the wolf Fenrir, the second was Jormungand, greatest of serpents, and the third was Hel. Even in a crowd of a thousand women Hel stood out. From the hips down every inch of Hel's body was decayed, and her expression was always the same – gloomy and grim.'

'More, tell us more,' Francine encouraged. Her driving had relaxed and steadied into a more even speed. Jake closed his eyes. He'd heard the exact same stories two years before.

'When the gods heard that Loki had fathered these children they were filled with alarm. They discussed what to do about them at the Well of Urd.

'"Their mother is evil," said Fate.

'"But their father is worse," Being said.

'"Expect nothing from them but the worst," said Necessity. "Expect them to harm you and endanger you."

'So the Gods agreed that Loki's children must be captured. One night they burst into Angrboda's hall and gagged and bound her before she had even rubbed her eyes; then they kidnapped her children and carried them back to Asgard.'

'Poor old Angrboda,' Francine said.

'Mum! Don't encourage her,' Jake protested, and he stretched out on the back seat and fell asleep.

Liza and Sam lived in a barn in Suffolk. Sam had built a gallery around the edge so that Libby could go to bed behind a railed-in curtain, and as soon as they arrived, Liza led them up the rickety stairs. 'The journey was terrible,' Francine shook her head, and outside the barn in great white folds the mist rolled and clung a foot above the ground. It had fallen on them the moment they crossed the county border. They'd seen the sign for Suffolk and they'd cheered, and then for hours and hours there was nothing else but white. Tess had woken twice to find her mother parked half on the verge, crying soft tears into the map, while the occasional passing headlight lit up the hopeless whiteness of the night.

'We thought you'd never make it,' Liza whispered, and she helped the children to crawl into the sleeping-bags she'd laid out on wooden bunks.

'Sleep tight,' Francine whispered as she stroked Tess's cheek, her hand all raised and veined from driving, and she followed Liza down into the cavernous room below for a sip of brandy and a sudden flush of hot exhausted tears.

'Happy Christmas,' Jake snarled as he thrashed and twisted in his zipped-up bag, and Tess lay awake listening to the mangled sounds of the grown-ups chattering and soothing, exclaiming and condemning, until Francine crept in to join them, tenderly unzipping Tess to slip a plastic sheet under her back.

'From Mummy and Daddy,' William sat cross-legged on the floor writing laboriously on little handmade cards. He turned and stared hard at Felicity who was lounging in the fireplace, her rounded belly tilted for comfort to one side, her loose hair, golden in the firelight, hanging half over her face. 'Tomorrow is meant to be a happy day,' he told her. 'Let's behave like grown-ups, shall we? Keep our problems to ourselves?' Felicity didn't answer. 'Right,' William went on, 'so for one thing, I don't want any mention of . . .' he found he couldn't say the name. 'I just don't want you upsetting the children. Do you understand?'

Felicity stayed unnaturally still. 'Yes,' she said, and he noticed there was a little well of blood rising up out of her lip. Without warning his heart looped up and softened for her. He had to clench his jaw and tell himself how she'd betrayed them. How she'd lived on in Cammothmore. Lived on in that wide open house that stretched towards the sea. Hung her coat against the crayon drawings in the hall, flung open the windows to lose the pee and biscuit smell, and worse than that, much worse, how she'd lain in the wooden bed he'd made for them, the wide low bed, the headboard carved and curled into a heart. She'd lain in that bed and conceived another child.

'So many presents,' Felicity said wonderingly, staring at the tree under which were piled the squares and rolls and twists of wrapping.

'We need spoiling,' William said, and Felicity raised an eyebrow to remark that the South was softening him, drawing him into its materialistic arms.

William picked needles off his corduroy knees. He used to like it when she teased him. It gave him a chance to tussle her around, and with a sudden optimism he began to crawl towards her, a twisted smile across his face to cover up the hurt. He thought what she was like when she was pregnant, round and hot with extra blood. Behind the angel curtain of her hair she grew big bodied and lush. He laid his hands down, catlike on the carpet, and Felicity swallowed, loud enough to hear. 'It's still there,' he thought, 'the old electricity.' And then he saw her hand move towards the fire. It closed over the poker and he stopped, drooping, as she smashed a log into the flames. William lowered his head and inspected the rug for needles. 'Well,' he yawned, rising to his feet, 'I expect we're in for an early start,' and he offered to show Felicity to her room.

'Will you be all right in here?' It seemed wrong to give her Francine's bed, but now that he was pointing to it, Tess's bottom bunk looked ridiculous and low.

'Fine.' Felicity sat down, and they both looked startled as the plastic sheet rustled under her weight.

'Good night, then,' William nodded, eager suddenly to be alone, and he wondered why a child of nine would still be wetting her bed. My children never had any such problems, even little Sandy goes through the night. With a surge of pleasure in this achievement he went up to his own room and slipped into a peaceful and self-righteous sleep.

The barn was bare and empty and for three days the mist hung round it like a shroud.

'Play with me,' begged Libby. 'Play with me, Tess.'

Jake held Tess by the arm. 'Let's see if we can find a phone box.' But she was frightened they'd get lost. If they walked out into the mist they might find themselves surrounded by bulls. Or they might fall into a river, one of many that gridded through the land, flat listless trenches that seemed to have no current on which to move. On Christmas afternoon, before the light gave out, Liza and Sam had taken them on a walk. They'd walked through fields and down a brambled lane, and then the mist had lifted to show a stretch of pebbled beach, and beyond it, rolling out for ever, was the sea.

'Let's find the sea again.' Jake pulled her, but Tess was frightened.

'No, Jake.' She saw he was determined and she held on to his coat. 'I'll tell you the story of how Loki had his mouth sewn shut.' It was the most grisly myth she knew. How the dwarves tried to stop Loki's ceaseless talking. They used an awl to pierce his lips and they sewed them tight together with a leather thong.

'Oh, all right then,' Jake gave in, and he sat beside Libby on the floor.

Doon's best present was a second guinea-pig. It was orange and white, its hair in whirls like the opening of a flower, and William had made a giant hutch for it with a room next door for Lupin to move in. 'One day they can have babies, but Daddy says it's too soon,' Doon told her mother.

Honour scowled and looked away.

'And then one of the babies can be my pet,' Sandy said. 'Daddy says I'm too little to have a pet just now.'

Felicity bent down. She stroked Sandy's baby head, the fine hair all tufted at the back. 'Have you thought of a name for her?' she asked Doon.

William stood up and tipped his tea into the sink. 'I gave up sugar five years ago, can you not remember that?'

Honour looked through the lenses of her glasses to see who would shout next.

But Felicity didn't shout. She straightened her shoulders, shook out her hair and put the kettle back on to the Rayburn to boil.

William's fingers twisted with frustration. Had he really frightened her so much? He hadn't meant to break her, just to punish her for what she did. Felicity stood and watched the kettle. Maybe she wasn't broken, William thought, maybe now without the children she simply felt restored.

'Mummy?' Doon slipped in close beside her. 'Mummy?' She clasped Felicity's fingers, lacing them through her own. 'Will you come and pick grass with me?'

'Of course.'

The other two girls sprang up. 'Me too.' They hung from her, pulling on her hands, her elbows and her arms, pushing their straggly heads against her hip. Only Honour looked back. She looked torn, as if she might still run to William, and he tried to will her, steer her to his side. But the younger children pulled Felicity towards the door, and Honour with a downward glance went too.

William followed at a distance and watched them through the hedge. He could see the four of them snapping up wet handfuls of grass, chatting and laughing like peasants at their work. It made him smile to watch them, and just as he was about to push himself through the hedge Felicity looked straight at him and gave him such a withering stare he stepped back into the road.

In the kitchen the kettle was jumping on the stove and

below its whistle he heard the low growl of Jake's cat. It was under the table, torturing a mouse, teasing it, taking slow pleasure in the fact that it still hadn't died. 'Odin!' William hissed and he kicked out, missed and slammed his toe against the edge of a bench. Odin bared his teeth and growled.

'Drop it, now.' He could see pink gums above pale yellow teeth, clenching tighter round the mouse, and with the animal spiked almost in two Odin leapt away and padded up the stairs. William hopped after him, and they ran from room to room in a clumsy childish chase. Odin skittered mockingly from window-sill to bed, jumped over a table and skidded through a pile of books. For a moment William thought he had him, his orange tail flicking just within his grasp, but the cat was doubling back, scooting out along the landing and disappearing down the stairs.

William slumped down on the floor. He could have cried with the pathetic waste of it. What was he doing here, lying face down in a mess of clothes and toys while his whole family was managing without him? He rolled over on to his back and tried to smile.

'If 'twas revenge that they were after
'Twas revenge that they had found
When they killed those little babies
And burned the cabin to the ground.'

It was a song that gave Doon bad dreams at night, the low

slow chronicle of the Red Indians taking their revenge on whites. It surprised him sometimes how much he liked the doomy tune of it.

'In olden times there was a river
Flowed between two mountain walls
And the people in the valley
Called that place the Haunted Falls.'

'Daddy, Daaaaaddy . . .' It was Sandy calling up the stairs. 'What's for supper?'

'Coming.' He struggled up, and with a sigh he went downstairs to roll out pastry for a flan.

Tess's heart skipped and shuddered as they drove over the cattle grid. 'We're back! We're back!' she shouted, squirming on the seat, and as they drew up she thought William had never looked so handsome. His hair seemed longer, falling into his eyes, and he had on a thick wool jumper like a child. He opened the door for Francine, and Tess, pressing down her handle, jumped out and ran to him. She wanted him to swing her round, feel his hands bite in under her arms, her feet lift off the ground, but instead he smiled distractedly and touched her head.

'Next Christmas,' she said, standing close and pulling at him, 'can we stay here with you?'

William looked at the Ford Anglia, still steaming and

shuddering from its long run. 'Yes, I don't see why not. Next Christmas. What do you think, Jake?'

Jake looked at him and narrowed his eyes. It was a look of the most withering disdain.

'I think we could have fun.' William moved to help Francine with the bags, and as their arms crossed over in the boot, a slow shy smile twisted Francine's face.

There was a rose-petal smell in their bedroom and Tess's pillow was all plumped. She lay down on her bed and breathed in.

'Christ,' Jake said, 'what kind of a stink is that?' He threw open both the windows. 'So . . .' he turned to Tess. 'What do you think? Poisoned or stabbed?'

'What?'

'Felicity. He may have cut her throat and buried her body in the wild. Didn't you think he had a sort of sinister look to him? I mean, even more than usual.'

'Oh, Jake!' Tess blushed. She thought he'd looked romantic with his hair in his eyes and his holiday jacket patched on both the arms.

'That leering grin he aimed at Mum.' Jake tilted his face into a grotesque but strangely accurate pose. 'I mean, do you think we should warn her? In case he tries to . . .' and Jake put his hands round his own throat and reeled around the room.

The rehearsals for *Oedipus*, the modern version, were put

on hold so that William could take his part in the teachers'
play. Every year, as close to Twelfth Night as they could
get, the teachers performed the tale of The Kings. There
was a fourth king, Herod, who wanted baby Jesus dead.
It was too frightening for the lower school, with devils,
murderers and hell, but the older children were allowed
to see it. Tess longed to watch. The hell mouth tattered,
dangling black, and the gate of heaven made from a million
pink flowers. 'Just think,' she said to Jake, 'next year you'll
be old enough to see the play.' And she shivered with the
thrill of it.

'Yippee,' Jake said in his most sarcastic voice, and Tess
wondered if when the Devil flipped his tail into his row
of seats he'd still be so unafraid.

Dear Dad,

We're back at The Wild and Odin is in disgrace because
he left a mouse, a dead one, on William's pillow. I think he
missed Jake because he's all thin and matted. We bought
him a new flea collar for Christmas, a red one instead of
green. I hope it works. Jake says will you call on Saturday
at seven minutes past six? Hope you're well. I'm very
well.

Love Tess.

William was reading a book about the elements. The
particles of character that make up the spirit and the soul.
'Little children,' he said, 'are always sanguine.' He made

81

a wiggle with his hand. 'Like little fishes, darting from one thing to the next. So . . .' he looked around the table, 'Sandy is sanguine and so is Doon. Jake, on the other hand,' he squinted at him along the length of the bench, 'is choleric. Peppery and hot. A fiery kind of creature.' Jake scowled, but Tess thought that secretly he was probably pleased.

Honour leaned forward for her turn. 'Honour is, let me see, the intellect, cool, rational, thinking. I'll have to look that up.'

She blinked happily behind her glasses and took a long sip from her glass.

'What about Tess?' Francine asked.

'Phlegmatic,' William said without a pause. Tess gulped and the gritty skin of the potato she was eating caught against her throat. He didn't even look it up. Are you sure? she wanted to ask, and she knew phlegmatic meant slow. Slow and brown and stupid. She took up another spoonful of potato, and packed it into her mouth. William had told them they should chew their food one hundred times. Like Tibetans with their rice. But after fifteen chews there was no potato left. She took up more potato and tried to make it last, but soon she had to stop because Honour was clearing away the plates. 'Come on, slow-coach,' Francine laughed, and William closed his book.

*

Doon's new guinea-pig was called Delilah. She let it nuzzle up with Lupin for half an hour each day and they snuffled and squeaked and munched their food.

'Do you want to play with her?' she asked Tess, and Tess sat with Doon and Sandy on the floor of their room making little jumps and bridges with outstretched arms and legs.

'Do you want it to be a baby boy or girl?' Tess whispered, unable to contain the question, even though William was marking essays in the room next door.

'When Lupin and Delilah have babies,' Sandy cut in, 'there will be three long-haired ones and two short-haired ones.'

'No, silly!' Doon shoved her. 'When – '

A creaking floorboard on the landing shocked them into silence.

'A boy . . . No – a girl,' Doon whispered when the creak had died away. 'I don't know.'

'I think a girl,' Tess said, and she realized she wanted that baby for her own. 'It could be called Marigold.'

Doon looked all puffy suddenly and pale.

'Don't cry, stupid,' said Sandy, kicking her, and one of the guinea-pigs escaped from the enclosure of her legs.

That night Doon stuck a needle into Sandy's skin. She pressed it through the roof of her bunk, in between the diamonds of the wire and right through the thin mattress into Sandy's bottom. It pricked Sandy just as she was drifting off to sleep and she leapt up with a scream.

'What is it?' William rushed up the stairs to see. 'What is it?' He lifted Sandy down.

'Is there blood?' Sandy was white and thrilled and William held her up against the mirror where a tiny spot of red was proof there'd been a wound.

Doon lay silent and curled up in her bed. 'I hate her,' she said eventually, and she pulled back her pillow to show the needle and confess.

'What's this?' William saw the corner of Doon's photograph. Felicity, the sun behind her, in a cheap gold frame. It was a photo he had taken years ago when too much light had crept through the lens. There was a rainbow over half her hair and her face was shadowy and lost. 'You weren't even born when this was taken.' He shook his head at Doon, and unable to control himself he banged the frame hard against the wall. As soon as he'd done it he felt sorry. 'I'm confiscating this,' he told her, and he traced his fingers over the cracks of glass. Doon pulled the covers up over her head, and even Sandy was quiet.

'I think Felicity favours Doon,' William told Francine. 'It's upsetting for the others, and no good for Doon at all. It makes me wonder whether they really would be better off not seeing her at all.'

'Or seeing her more?' Francine tried to catch his eye.

William was frowning, looking at the floor. 'Impossible. She can't keep rushing up and down from Scotland. It costs a fortune, apart from anything else, and it's me who has to pay.'

'I just don't know . . .'

'Anyway, the court ruled twice a year, and they're the experts. They deal with this sort of thing all the time. Twice a year, they said, and they were the ones thinking of the welfare of each child.'

'But William . . . surely things change?'

William put up his hand to stop her. 'You weren't there.' A sudden tic flickered in his eye. 'You don't know what it was like when she walked out.'

Francine waited for the hurt to leave his face. 'Camomile tea?' she offered, giving him a smile. 'Or something stronger?'

'Thank you,' William agreed, and he cleared a huge pile of washing from the table to a chair.

William liked his costume. It was a skin-tight matt-black leotard and his tail was long enough to hang over his arm. He practised walking for his part in a kind of sideways saunter, knees nudging out to the side, and he hoped while he was rehearsing that the fear of his performance would leak into legend in the annals of the school. He would be so dazzling, so mesmerizing, so utterly sexily terrifying that when in the New Year he read Wordsworth to his A-level class they would be so transfixed they'd hardly dare draw breath.

One night after supper, four Class Twelve students came up for a drink. William had invited them to prove that just because he was a teacher it didn't mean he couldn't be their friend. 'Meet some of my cast,' he said and he smiled from ear to ear.

They all sat beside the fire and drank cider, giggling and promising they wouldn't tell, and all the children were allowed to stay up a bit longer than usual for a treat. There was Alison with her white-blonde hair curling in corkscrews like a lamb, and two darker girls with shiny noses and bangles on their arms. With them was a boy called Simon, serious and stooped, his hair dark brown and lank over his ears. The girls all had tight jeans on and their legs swelled and overlapped as they lounged on cushions on the floor. Alison picked up William's guitar and strummed and hummed in a sweet drawly voice. 'Do you play?' she asked when William came in with glasses, and he looked all shy and said he'd taught himself.

'To impress the women,' Francine whispered, and the three girls blushed and laughed and looked away from his long legs.

The next day during lunch-hour Tess overheard them as they walked around the rhododendron island. 'Poor old Wooden Willy,' one of them laughed. 'Do you think he buys his trousers from a special shop?'

'Maybe he orders them from a catalogue.'

'Or alters them specially to get that extra snug fit.'

'Extraordinarily snug fit, you mean.'

The three girls, their arms linked, their knees knocking, folded up with laughter. 'Wooden Willy, Wooden Will,' they choked, and they dived into the bushes for a cigarette.

Tess and Jake sat on the bench outside the phone box and heard the village clock chime quarter past six. It was dark and silent and they hardly dared talk in case they missed the ringing.

'Did you have something you wanted to ask?'

'Shhh,' Jake started in case they'd missed that first vibration right before the ring. Sometimes if you were hovering you could pick it up almost as they dialled.

'Yes,' he said eventually, and the clock chimed out the half.

'I expect he's busy,' said Tess. 'He might be working, or out somewhere with Georgina.'

'Yes,' said Jake and slowly they trudged back up the hill.

That night Tess woke in a welter of bad dreams. Her bed was cold and wet. She peeled off her nightdress and tiptoed through to the next room. The curtains were not drawn and through the window the moon shone down and lit up her white body as she climbed. 'Mum . . .' she whispered, and as she slid in under the cover she came up against an unfamiliar arm. Bony, smelling bitter-sweet of sweat. Tess froze. She held her breath as she slithered out again, her toes feeling for the floor. Within seconds she was back in her room. She could hear the loud rough purr of Odin, sleeping curled in against Jake's side.

Quickly she pulled out the bottom sheet, and bundling it into a ball with the wet part in the centre, she climbed in between the top sheet and the blanket. With Odin's low hum like an engine, purring through the mattress over her head, she drifted back to sleep.

The next morning at breakfast Tess avoided the eye of the Class Twelve student whose white flesh she'd momentarily touched.

'Simon just dropped round for a chat.' William looked proud. 'And suddenly it was too late for him to get home. More porridge, Simon?'

'No thanks, Mr . . . I mean William,' Simon said, and he laughed uncomfortably with the newness of the name.

'I hope your parents won't have worried.' William frowned and then he looked Simon over and told him how at nineteen he'd been marching round the country, supporting the workers in their strikes. 'A year later I was married,' he said, 'and six months after that Honour was born.' He winked at Simon and Simon blushed bright red.

William leant towards the awkward, timid face. 'Do you have plans? Do you?' But instead of listening to the answer, a great wheel of possibilities began to spin. I'm still young, he told himself. I'm still so young, there's nothing I can't do. So that by the time Simon had finished outlining his plans to work with the forestry commission in New Zealand, William had to nod and pretend he'd heard a single word.

'But it's freezing,' Jake complained. Honour was already waiting in her mac.

William fixed Jake with a stern look. 'It'll do you good. A bit of adventure. Feel the wind in your hair. Test your wits. Make you into a man.'

'It's only a reservoir, not the Atlantic Ocean.' Jake slumped off to get his coat. 'Don't get carried away.'

'Can I come, please, I'd love to go sailing.'

William looked down at his shoes, blue and white canvas as if he owned a Riviera yacht. He didn't want to take Tess.

'Please. Please!'

But it seemed senseless to leave behind the only person who actually wanted to go.

The sky was steely and the water of the reservoir was ruffled with the wind. Tess's teeth began to chatter. She'd never been in a boat before and as soon as she was in and the wind filled out the sail, she knew she didn't like it.

'Duck your heads!' William shouted as the boom shot across, just missing Honour. William struggled and pulled to get control of the little boat, hired along with life-jackets from the yachting club. 'Let out the mainsail,' he roared as the boom swept back again. There was water in the bottom of the boat and Tess's plimsolls were already wet. 'Starboard!' William shouted and they scrambled to join him on his side, sitting high up on the tilting edge as the wind whipped up great flecks of foam.

'Can we go in soon?' Honour asked. Her face was ashen, her nose bright red with cold, but William was elated.

'Just once more round the lake,' he said, and as he stood up to man the rudder the small boat spun and juddered and he had lean out over the side with all his weight to stop it going down.

'Wasn't that wonderful?' They'd finally heaved the boat on to dry land. 'We'll come again next Saturday.'

With soaking feet and icy hands they followed him into the boat-house, where the bar that sometimes sold hot chocolate was closed due to the bad weather that had kept everyone else at home.

'Can I come again next Saturday too?' Tess asked.

William looked at her suspiciously. 'We'll come every weekend.'

'Great,' she said, and she shivered with dread.

I'll sell The Wild and buy a boat, William thought to himself as he sat at his desk, marking an essay he had set for homework. 'Dionysus and Apollo.' We'll sail around the world. I'll teach the children myself, have lessons up on deck. He stood up and stared out of the window. He could see the foundations of the garage and the jutting of one wall covered in bright plastic to keep off the rain. I'll have to finish the garage first. Build the chicken coop, tidy up the wild, and then I'll pay off the mortgage and set sail.

There was a light tapping on the door. 'Yes. What is it?' The children, at least his children, knew he wasn't to be disturbed.

Francine opened the door and silently offered in a cup of tea. 'Don't work too late.'

'No.' He looked up from his desk. There was only one more essay to mark. It had a huge shaded heading, DIONYSUS in bright reds and yellows, APOLLO in ice-blue. He could see this student was just trying to use up space. 'I won't.' He took the tea out of Francine's hand, and as he did so he felt a surge of energy, and although he knew he shouldn't, he took her other hand and drew her into the room. 'You're not fair on me,' he told her.

'What do you mean?' She looked startled as if he was about to ask her to move out.

William moved nearer and let his mouth brush against her ear. 'You're too beautiful,' he said. 'Too beautiful to resist,' and he stepped backwards with her until laughing they fell on to his bed.

I mustn't get entangled, he thought as he pulled her up against him. Mustn't get involved. And he thought of the boat he'd buy, the prow of it arching through white waves, while his children learnt to crew and cook and scribble essays on the rolling deck.

'Tess!' Jake pulled her arm. 'Look!' It was Victor's oil-blue car gliding smoothly up the hill. As they watched, the wheels trilled over the cattle grid and the car disappeared among the trees. 'We'll catch him up!' They ran across the road and through the side gate, scratching their clothes as they pushed through the wild. They jumped out on Victor as he walked up the ramp, his black shoes slipping on the wooden planks.

'Hello,' he smiled. Georgina wasn't with him and he looked breezy and aloof.

'Come in, come in.' Jake led him in triumph into the kitchen where William's three girls were just kicking off their shoes. 'Muuuuum!' Jake shouted, and Francine appeared from the laundry room.

'Victor,' she frowned, then dipped her head and smiled. 'What –? I mean . . .' Tess could see her struggling. 'Would you like a drink of anything?'

'No, thanks.' He was holding on to the rail of the Rayburn and he looked springy, as if there was hardly any weight on his feet. His coat was grey, his suit silvery black, and everything about him was sleek and ironed and clean.

Honour, Doon and Sandy stood and stared at him. Their cheeks were reddened, their hair frizzled from the wind. Tess looked at her hands, earth from the garden wedged under the nails, rough skin and tiny hair-line cuts from climbing trees. Even her mother had bobbles on her tights and there was a dry leaf in her hair.

'Please have a cup of tea,' Francine said. 'You're making me nervous.'

'Of course.' Victor darted his eyes over the children, jolting them for a second out of their trance. Only Jake was moving. Holding tight on to Odin, dancing up and down on his toes.

'Excuse me.' Francine had to nudge in beside him to slip the kettle on to the stove.

'Oh, I'm sorry,' he said, but he only moved an inch.

'Dad, Dad.' Jake had him by the arm. 'I want to show you something.'

Tess stood back against the wall to let them pass and she heard Jake from a distance, breathless from explaining how fierce, rare, and endangered some of his favourite animals were. She waited in the kitchen, checking her name on the rota, glancing across the whole month's chores for brown. It was her turn to help with supper. 'What are we having, Mum?'

'Well . . .' There were potatoes, parsnips, carrots and a huge old turnip that needed to be used up. 'I thought I'd make soup.' Francine turned the cold tap on and started gouging mud out of the dents and eyes. Honour sidled up the stairs to do her violin practice.

'Where's Daddy?' Sandy clung round Francine's legs.

'He's rehearsing his play,' Francine said. 'Doon, why don't you two both go upstairs?'

'I have to pick grass.' But instead of going out Doon hovered by the door. Tess stood beside her and together they watched Victor flicking through Jake's letters, a prized collection personally signed by Cyril Littlewood of the World Wildlife Fund.

Dear Jake,

How lovely to hear from you again. Yes, I did get your painting of a giraffe. It was most unusual and very atmospheric. I think it's a wonderful idea, a sponsored walk, but maybe wait until the spring?

'Where would you walk?' Victor asked.

'Along the old railway line. I did it before. We raised twenty-eight pounds.'

'That's a fortune.' Victor put the letters down, very gently, almost apologetic. 'I should just have a word with your mother.' He sidled out, past Jake, past Doon and Tess huddled and watchful by the back door, and into the kitchen where Francine was leaning over the sink.

'Listen,' Victor tried to turn Francine towards him with his voice. 'I've come into a bit of money. Someone wants to publish a collection of my stories. I know how difficult things have been – but – well, if you still wanted I could help you find somewhere . . .'

Francine kept her chin down. Her hands stayed motion-less in the sink. After a moment, when neither of them spoke, Francine dried her hands.

'I mean, really,' Victor lowered his voice, 'you can't live here.'

Francine looked at him. 'I can live here,' she said. 'You'd be surprised.' She blinked fast and turned back to the swampy sink, the tops and tails of carrots floating in the mud.

'But Dad,' Tess wanted to show him what The Wild was really like, 'did you know we've got a washing machine? And you haven't seen the badminton court yet.' She pulled him outside where the net was flapping in the wintry dark. 'You can't really see, but William has marked the boundaries out in white. It's the best place here, it really is. We can walk up on to the forest, and Mum's teaching us all how to sew.'

'Really?' Victor sighed and he squeezed Tess's hand.

Victor didn't wait for William to get home. He ate a bowl of lumpy country soup and then slipped back into his car. Jake jumped into the back. He let his body slide along the silken seat, pulled out the ashtrays and made faces in the mirror. 'Can we visit you in London?' he asked.

'Of course. Of course you can.' Victor turned and looked at Francine. 'Think about what I've said?'

Francine shook her head. 'No,' she said, smiling, and they laughed at each other as he reversed out.

Felicity wrote to the children.

'Dear Honour, Doon and Sandy,' Honour read the letter, her fingers trembling, her glasses pinching red against her nose. 'You have a little brother.' She stopped, and Sandy gasped, her mouth falling so far open you could see her tonsils drooping at the back. 'His name is Abraham. He's got some dark fluffy hair and a VERY large willy.' Tess put her fingers in her mouth to stop the laugh. 'I'll send a photo of him soon. In the meantime I miss you and I love you all so much. Mummy.'

'That's wonderful.' Francine's eyes were misty with the memory of Jake. 'A little boy.'

William stood up to slice more bread. He sliced and sliced until the whole long loaf was gone. 'Abraham!' he snorted. 'How's that going to fit in in Cammothmore?'

'That's enough bread, I think.' Francine took the knife out of his hands. 'Does anyone want more toast?'

'The bitch,' William muttered.

But no one did want toast.

That Easter William's brother, Alec, came to stay. Whenever William talked about his brother, his whole face darkened and his eyes turned thin as slits. 'Alec only ever had three interests,' William told them. 'Motorbikes, music and girls.' He looked round the table to see if everyone had understood. 'All impossible for him now.'

'Why music?' Francine asked, and Tess was relieved because she had been about to ask, 'Why girls?'

'His hearing got damaged in the crash,' William said, his eyebrows knitting as if the mangled metal of Alec's bike were cutting in there now. 'Now the high notes hurt him, and he has to adjust his hearing aid to manage the pain.' William looked warningly at Sandy who had a high squeak of a voice. High, and quite astonishingly loud.

'But he's still very independent?' Francine prompted and William breathed in so deeply that his chest began to dent towards his shoulders and he had to yawn to breathe back out. 'Yes,' he said. 'Yes, that's right, he is. He's coming on the train, although I offered to drive up and get him. But no, he said he didn't want to be stuck on the motorway for two hours with me. The British Rail guards' van, he said, would be preferable to that.' William laughed sadly and his daughters, as if to cheer him up, laughed too.

Alec's wheelchair skidded on the ramp. 'No,' he raised an arm against his brother's helping hands. 'I'll manage,' and William had to content himself with walking close behind while Alec pushed with all his strength against the wheels.

Tess watched as he heaved himself up. He looked like William, with the same slug of a nose, and eyes jet black and narrow, but his arms in his cap-sleeved T-shirt were huge and veined, and there was no gold in his hair. Tess could see the blue blood knotted behind the skin and the tight sheen of the muscles bulging as he wheeled. William looked spindly behind him, his woollen jumper loose around his waist, his silken hair hanging into his eyes. Alec wheeled himself across the garden and in through the front door.

'So who likes chocolate?' He braked sharp with a flourish, and the children gathered round, trying not to stare at the spokes and tubes and wires that seemed to link him to his chair. 'I hear no one in this house likes chocolate, is that, right?'

'We do, we do!' Everyone rushed to contradict him and even Jake held out his hand. 'I do!' Sandy shrieked, and Alec's hearing aid screamed and span. He winced with pain, grasping and twisting with thick fingers, twisting until the dial was down.

'All right.' A film of sweat stood out on his forehead. 'Christ, Will.' He looked up at William, hovering by the rota. 'It's like living in a zoo. How did you get so many wee ones, you frisky hound?'

William watched anxiously as Alec unzipped a small black bag and handed out the sweets. There were Caramac bars, peanut brittle, wine gums and Pink Panther chocolate that turned to milk syrup in your mouth. 'That's enough now, I think.' William was nervous. Usually if there was chocolate, it was shared out, exactly one square each. 'Come on now Alec, you don't want them to be sick.'

'Thank you Alec, thank you.' Honour wrapped up the remainder of her Milky Way. 'I'll save it for later.' William gave her an approving look.

'Thank you, thank you,' the others chimed and William held a hand tight over Sandy's mouth.

Alec winked at the children. 'They'll survive,' he said. 'Just relax, can't you, Will?' He handed him a rolled-up scroll of paper, poster sized with brown letters against cream. '*The Desiderata*,' William read unrolling it, and all down the page was a long prose poem of advice.

Go placidly amid the noise and haste, and remember what peace there may be in silence.

Alec raised his eyebrows at William.

As far as possible without surrender be on good terms with all persons. Speak your truth quietly and clearly; and listen to others, even the dull and ignorant; they too have their story.

'Thank you, Alec.' William breathed deeply, and even though he knew it was his turn for supper he checked the rota for his name.

'I'll put it up here,' Honour volunteered, and she found

the Sellotape in its drawer and stretched up to stick *The Desiderata* to the wall above the Rayburn.

Alec was in the last laps of a race. His bike was speeding on ahead when just behind him another bike skidded off the track and crashed into a pole. The pole was cushioned with soft bales of hay and Alec saw the other driver, a flicker in the corner of his eye, get up and walk away. But Alec was winning, rushing on to victory, his fifth win in a row, and he didn't expect it when on the very last lap he hit the exact same slick of mud. His bike reared up, red hot, an enemy before him, and he could see that pole, the bales of hay flung clear. The pole was hurtling towards him, and in the second just before his body snapped he knew his life was gone. But what William found unnerving was how Alec never complained about the hay. He never cursed those bales, and the men who'd had no time to put them back. What he complained about was that no one ever told him he didn't always have to win. He'd been stupid. Stupid and unlucky. Stupid to push himself in such an unimportant race, and unlucky not to die.

Alec wanted to take William and Francine to Brands Hatch. 'We're not far away,' he said. 'It's a waste not to go.' He wheeled himself down to the phone box to call some of his old biker friends.

'They don't really like to see me,' he told them when the tickets were sent through. 'It makes them edgy having a cripple so close by. But we're going all the same. We'll drink champagne and sit in the members' enclosure. Of course they don't have fucking wheelchair access but you and Frankie can carry me up the stairs.'

'Of course we can.' Francine flexed her own slim arms and William nodded from the far end of the room.

There was still one thing apart from bikes and girls and music that Alec liked to do, and that was welding. He sat in the conservatory with a tiny soldering iron and made a puzzle out of copper bars. The puzzle was a mesh of metal rings and triangles. One ring, he insisted, unattached itself from the others and unlocked the chain. If you were clever enough you'd see easily how it was done. Tess took the puzzle into her room. She would unfold the secret of it and both Alec and William would be amazed. She dangled it and twisted it and pulled at all the lines, but however hard she tried it was impossible to do. 'Please show me, Alec,' she begged, but Alec only smiled and passed it to Honour, who with all her brains couldn't begin to work it out. Even William had a go. He sat and looked at it for a long time. 'I've got it,' he said and he gritted his teeth as he pulled the circle round.

'No,' Alec beamed when the ring refused to unlock and William jangled it down on to the table.

'I'd better get on,' William said, irritably pushing up his sleeves, and he went to mix more concrete for the garage floor.

Jake was the only one who didn't care about the puzzle. He sat beside Alec at the corner of the table and wrinkled his nose against his smell.

'It's hard being the only boy,' Alec smiled sympathetically when Jake declined to try the puzzle. 'I should know,' and he nodded towards William, who raised his fist at him and stuck out his tongue.

William laid the cement floor, built the bricks up to the next level, and when there was no more he could do, he took his chainsaw and began to clear the wild.

'Not this one, please.' Tess climbed up the nail steps she'd banged into her favourite tree and hung from the first branch. William pulled off his jacket. He stood straight and looked around, and then holding the sharp teeth of the chainsaw away from him began clearing the undergrowth. When he stopped he didn't pause to rest. 'Who wants a game of badminton?' he challenged, and he forced Honour away from her Easter homework and thrashed the shuttlecock down into her court.

Alec watched them from the conservatory, where he sat bent over a small blue flame. He was making earrings for Francine, flowers curled out of twists of copper wire. 'You've got a sparkler there,' he told William so everyone could hear, and William shook his head, warning him to stop.

'He's blushing!' Alec teased, and it was true, William's face had darkened red.

Francine looked up. Her eyes were soft and warm. 'Alec!' she scolded, and the children watched as she pulled back her hair to hold an earring up against her ear.

On the last day of Alec's stay William switched off his chainsaw. He oiled the teeth and cleaned the grooves and packed it carefully away. He washed clean his bricklaying palette and rinsed away the sand, and when Alec was safely at the station he sank down into the cushions of the fireplace and didn't move.

'Supper's ready,' Francine called to him.

'I don't think I will.'

He was still there when the children went to bed that night, and Honour tried to soothe him with a song. She sang him one of his own favourites.

'I wish I was a lizard in the spring,
I wish I was a lizard in the spring.
If I was a lizard in the spring,
I'd hear my darling sing.
I wish I was a lizard in the spring.'

It sounded cold without the guitar, and when he thanked her his smile was thin.

'Was William there when Alec crashed?' Tess asked as Francine tucked her in.

'No, no, he wasn't. Thank God.'

'It's just . . . I was wondering if it was the same explosion that made William's ear go deaf.'

Francine started to laugh. 'It wasn't an explosion. He injured his ear with a cotton bud, pushing it in too far.'

'Oh,' Tess said, and the image of the cotton bud popping into William's head was somehow worse than anything she'd thought. 'No one did Alec's puzzle,' she remembered then.

'It wasn't a puzzle,' Jake said. He was stroking Odin so swift and hard his purr was like a roar. 'It was a trick and everyone was too polite to see it. There was no link in the chain and Alec was waiting to see if anyone would guess.'

'Jake.' Francine patted his bed, but Tess knew that he was right.

Mr Paul perched for a moment on his desk, resting his weight on the ridge of wood. 'Now who gave birth to a son nine months after Heimdall's visit?'

'Affi and Amma,' Class Four chorused back.

'Yes,' Mr Paul smiled. 'The boy's cheeks were ruddy, he had bright eyes, and Affi and Amma called him Karl. Karl was quick to grow and he was well built and strong.

When Karl was a young man his parents found him a wife. Her name was Snor. They exchanged rings and laid a bright counterpane on their bed. Karl and Snor had a cluster of contented children. They called their first-born Man, and their second Warrior. Their other sons were Landowner, Thane and Smith, who was a master of every craft, Broad Shoulders, Yeoman and Clipped Beard, Bui and Boddi, Brattskegg and Segg. Karl and Snor also had daughters. Their eldest they called Snot the Serving Woman. There was Bride and Swan-Neck and Proud, Fair and Womanly and Sprund. Vif was born to make a good wife, Feima was bashful, and Ristil, the youngest, was graceful as any woman. These were the children of Karl and Snor and from them stem the race of peasants.'

'Go away. It's private,' Jake scowled as he pulled Tess after him into the phone box. Tess stood with her face pressed against the glass and watched the Strachan girls trail obediently up the hill. They didn't look back until they reached the very top, and when they did Jake seized the receiver and babbled into it, although Honour, even with her glasses, couldn't possibly see anything from there.

'Maybe Dad's too busy working,' he said when finally the girls were out of sight.

'Yes, or gone on holiday.'

'Don't be silly. I think we should visit. He said we should.'

'To London?'

'Yes.'

Tess squeezed out of the phone box. They'd been to London on their own before. Francine had put them on the train and Victor had met them at Victoria station. Once they'd caught a bus with him to Maida Vale. They'd come out of the train station, turned to the left, and there at the third bus stop was a number sixteen bus.

'I know the way,' Jake said. 'We get off at Harrow Road. Walk to the cake shop and then it's the second road on the right.'

Tess remembered the cake shop. It was full of white and yellow sponge, pink icing and frilly looking cream. There was nothing homemade, with dark-brown flour or dates.

'We'll go one Saturday.'

'But what about sailing?'

Jake snorted. 'Write and tell him that we're coming.'

'All right.' Tess wanted to ask him why he never wrote himself, but she knew it was because of spelling. The teachers at school said spelling didn't necessarily matter, but Tess knew Jake was ashamed. At George House it was the imagination that was important and Jake's use of colour, apparently, was superb. Last year his woodwork and metalwork reports were brilliant. At home Francine had tried to help him, sounding out the words with him for hours at a time, but her prompting sent him into a fury and he'd lose control and want to tear the book. 'Be patient, Jake, it'll come,' Francine had tried to soothe him, and even though William was a teacher he didn't seem to have any idea of how to help. 'Honour just seemed to pick it up.' He had to look away, because when he thought of Honour and her cleverness, he felt a flush of pride. It eclipsed the fact that Doon retained nothing and cried great silent tears when he tried to teach her how to tell the time. William had always talked quite openly with Honour. He trusted her intelligence to understand. At bath time he'd explained to her their sexual differences, listing the different words for his and hers. At night time he'd pointed out the planets, Venus and Mars, and the constellations of the stars. He'd explained the phases of the moon and how when she grew into a woman they'd pull the blood inside her back and forwards like a tide. He'd talked to her about his work, his projects, his interest in ancient history, and it was one of his great delights how easily, how neatly and seriously, she packed everything away. It had been easy to talk to her about Felicity, explaining to her just how her mother had let everybody down. She'd been selfish, childish, deceitful and disloyal, and it was important these were things that Honour knew.

Photographs of the baby Abraham arrived, grainy black and white pictures as big as a page. William refused to look at them but later Tess saw him frowning into the baby's huge brown eyes. Doon was allowed to Sellotape the photographs to her wall. Honour had bookshelves beside her bed laden with the classics, and Sandy had a collection of multi-coloured snot. Brown, green, yellow and orange, all dried into smears and tiny ropes of string. It was her Bogey Collection, small but growing, there to replace the one she'd left behind. 'If no one else wants Abraham I'll have him,' Doon said, and she kissed the baby mouth before she went to sleep.

We must improve our lives, William thought as he smashed his axe into a log. The wood was green with lichen, and toadstools grew along it like a little hill of roofs. We'll become vegetarians, he decided. Sprinkle wheatgerm over our muesli, however bitter it tastes. And then something occurred to him, something that seemed the obvious thing to do. He'd buy Honour a dog.

'A gentle dog with no interest in sheep,' Mr Jenkinshaw advised him, and William felt proud to think that he'd befriended this old man, a real man of the country, maybe the last of his tribe. He lived cut off from everyone in the last uncultivated part of forest, and stretched around him on every side was a bright green sea of golf. The golfers had to skirt around his garden, they lost their balls in the thicket of his fence, but no one, however much they offered, had been able to convince him to move on. 'A Labrador,' Mr Jenkinshaw suggested. A Labrador.

William couldn't help but feel deflated. He'd always thought of Labradors as carpet-slipper dogs. 'Nice and friendly for a little girl,' Mr Jenkinshaw nodded, and he glanced musingly over his smallholding and said he'd better be getting on.

A week later William found a puppy. A black Labrador born on the biodynamic farm. He couldn't believe the luck of it. The dog was bound to be superior, raised as it was on organic meat and slops from vegetables sown at night time in conjunction with the moon. The dog was male with a large head and heavy paws. It looked bafflingly stupid. William bent down to it and found it looking up at him with idiotic devotion in its eyes.

Tess threw a ball against the half-built wall of the garage. She clapped, turned and caught the ball under her leg. She had to try and reach a hundred. If she reached a hundred a letter would come. 'Yes,' she could tell Jake and then she could stop watching him fumble every morning for the post.

'Seventy-eight, seventy-nine,' as long as she didn't drop the ball, and then William's van swung into the drive and she forgot about her father and the letter and ran to meet him at the bottom of the ramp.

'William!' When he saw her he pushed the small warm dog inside his coat. 'William, guess what? Lupin and Delilah have had babies. Millions of them. They chewed through the wall. They must have been visiting each other for weeks!'

William felt his shoulders sag. 'Oh, I see.'

'It's so exciting. And they all look like Delilah, not a single long-haired one. Doon says she wants to keep them all.'

William frowned. He pushed past Tess into the house, where with a flourish he presented the small black dog to Honour, who jumped back startled as if she'd had a fright.

'Can I keep the guinea-pigs? Can I?' Doon had tears ready in her eyes.

'I don't see why not,' William told her, and delighted she ran outside to give Delilah the good news.

'Are you sure about London?' Francine turned to Jake and scrutinized him.

'Yes, Dad wants us to visit him. He says he'll meet us at Victoria just after twelve.'

'I'm not sure if I've got . . .'

'It's all right.' Jake stopped her. 'We've got money for the train.'

Francine stirred a huge cauldron of lentils, breaking up the whole tomatoes with a spoon. 'But Jake?' Francine added a bayleaf and a sprinkling of salt. She looked pale and a little worried. 'Have you fed the cat? It's just he's been terrorizing the guinea-pigs, hissing at them through the wire.'

'Odin!' Jake opened a tin of Whiskas on the doorstep so the smell of it would lure him into the house. 'King of the Cats,' he nuzzled when Odin finally brushed in, his coat glistening, his eyes shining from the dark. Jake picked him up and pressed his cheek against his fur.

There were ten stations between East Grinstead and Victoria. Tess knew them off by heart. Dormans. Lingfield. Hurst Green. Oxted. Woldingham. Upper Warlingham. Riddles Down. Sanderstead. East Croydon. Clapham Junction, and Victoria.

'We come out of the station, turn left, take the number sixteen bus, get off after the flyover, walk to the cake shop, turn left, then right . . .' Tess wasn't sure what number it was but Victor's door was black. It had a brass knocker and a letterbox with a grille behind it to collect the post.

'We come out of the station, turn left, take the number sixteen bus . . .' Jake practised from the top bunk, but then Francine came in and stood forlornly by the door.

'I don't think London's a good idea,' she said, stooping slightly as if to absorb Jake's rage. 'William feels . . . well, when I mentioned it to him, he said the problem with it is that it's not fair.'

Jake didn't move. He levelled her with an ice-cold stare. 'Life's not fair,' he said.

Francine smiled and shook her head. 'I'm sorry.' She reached up to stroke Jake's head. 'Another time.' She kissed Tess on the cheek and slowly, apologetically, closed the door.

'What shall we do now?' Jake thumped his head into the pillow.

'Well . . .' Tess wasn't sure. 'It's not as if Dad was actually expecting us.'

'Who's side are you on?' he hissed and they lay like that in silence until Jake said, 'I hope we move again soon.'

'Yes,' Tess said to cheer him up. 'I expect we will.'

'It is fair!' Jake suddenly leapt out of bed. 'It is fair because of Honour's dog.'

Tess battled up out of her dream. The cliff was splitting and she was running along one single splintering ledge. She jumped across a chasm and then suddenly she was awake.

'Jake, don't!' She tried to grab at his pyjamas but he was already running for the door.

'We're going,' he said a minute later, brushing past her and vaulting back into his bed. 'I've told them we'll go this Saturday,' and he sighed happily and fell asleep.

Honour named her dog Spotless for the simple reason that he didn't have any spots. No spots except above his eyes, where there were two smooth ovals of brown fur.

They were like eyebrows, ruffled and surprised, and when he raised his ears they knitted together in a frown. 'That's not pure Labrador,' Mr Jenkinshaw told William when they took Spotless out for his first walk. The dog wrinkled his brow and cocked his head to one side. 'I'm warning you,' Mr Jenkinshaw sighed, 'you'd better watch out for that dog. There's sheepdog, Labrador and Doberman.' Mr Jenkinshaw shook his head. 'You'll find that dog's no good,' he said, and walked away.

Spotless was a nuisance. He chewed the leg off William's chair, and in three minutes while Francine was pulling up a lettuce, he ate a family-sized tray of cauliflower cheese. William built a gate to keep him in the kitchen, but after one trial jump he leapt right over it, landing in a huddle on the wooden floor. Before anyone could catch him he'd raised his leg to wee into the fire. 'Spotless! Spotless!' Honour searched the house for him until she realized he'd shrunk his body into an elongated arch and squeezed out through the cat flap. 'Spotless!' She strained with the effort to control him. 'Help, someone!' She clung to the dog's collar before he broke free and bounded off to explore the field of sheep across the road behind the house.

William put up a wire fence, and when Spotless jumped over it, he added an extra-high extension to the top. 'It's like living in Colditz,' Jake muttered, and Francine planted sweet peas and runner beans to soften the grey wire.

Oxted, Woldingham, Upper Warlingham, Riddles Down, Sanderstead, East Croydon . . . Clapham Junction . . . and they were there, surrounded by the roar of Victoria, people pushing, announcements crackling, and the gritty, dirty, exhilarating smell of grime. Jake took hold of Tess's hand. Turn left out of the station, that's what they'd planned. But today there didn't seem to be a left. They pushed on through the crowd, pressed themselves against the walls, but hard as they looked there didn't seem to be an opening to the left. The left, the left, Jake squinted, but whichever way they went they kept being forced round to the right. Tess stopped and looked up into the roof. There were stripes of light, spokes and clocks and pigeons spinning round. Someone bumped against her and a suitcase hit her arm.

'Excuse me,' Jake was asking someone. A smart woman in a raincoat. 'Do you know how we get to Harrow Road?'

'Harrow?' The woman frowned. 'You'll have to get the tube.'

'We were going to get the bus . . .'

'Harrow on the Hill.' The woman closed her eyes. She had a ticket clutched tightly in her hand. 'Yes, that's it. Come on, I'll show you where the train leaves from.' She took Jake's arm and bustled off and Tess pressed herself against his back and scurried to keep up.

'Harrow. Harrow Road?' Jake said hopefully as the woman held out her hand for money. 'Two half-fare tickets, yes,' she said and she passed over precious money for their fares. Then she pointed them along a dingy tunnel and told them to get the first train that came in. Tess was certain she was wrong, but the woman watched them walking away and when they turned, she waved them on.

Jake and Tess sat together, tense and silent as the train swished closed its doors. It was just possible Harrow on the Hill was near the flyover on Harrow Road, right beside the cake shop. They'd get off there and walk straight into their father's road. But they were passing through so many stations, each one with a less familiar name, and then the train rumbled up above the ground. There were trees and parks and long back gardens and some of the people who got on knew each other's names. 'Oh God,' Jake groaned and Tess felt near despair. 'It isn't even London.'

Eventually they arrived at Harrow on the Hill. It was a small suburb like East Grinstead, with sky and trees and breeze. Jake was pale with shame. He pulled Tess's arm and led her straight across the bridge to the other platform and back on to another train. Victoria, the sign said, and they sat in silence until they arrived. This time they didn't dare ask for directions and after half an hour of trailing round the pillars, arches and side-streets of the station, they found the row of bus stops and a magical sign that said 16.

*

'Dad, Dad,' they called. 'Daaad!' they shouted, banging with the knocker and ringing the bell. There were great scars on the door like giant fingernails and in white letters words were scrawled and half rubbed out.

'Baa . . . rnstand,' Jake read.

'Bastard, I think,' said Tess.

Victor opened the door. 'Hello.' He looked surprised to see them. 'Is it Saturday?' he said then.

'Yes,' Tess said.

'So, what are you two up to?' He smiled as if they might be simply on a jaunty day out. Jake and Tess stared at him. They felt too shy to know what to do. 'Come in.' They followed him up the stairs, scuffing the bare boards, kicking at the nails. Victor had the middle flat of a large white house. There was a kitchen, a bedroom, and through wide open wooden doors a bathroom where the bath stood alone in the middle of the floor. The bath embarrassed Tess. Magazines and newspapers lay three deep beside it. There were coffee cups and papers, and even the telephone was stretched towards it on a lead.

The other rooms in comparison looked empty. The kitchen was stark, with one small dented saucepan on the stove. In the bedroom there was a metal bed, an armchair, and under the window a huge desk, strewn with papers, typed on, scrawled over and crossed out. On the very edge of the desk, jammed against the window, was a tottering pile of pages. Jake stood admiringly beside it, measuring it with his eyes, letting his fingers trail over its edges.

'How's Georgina?' Tess asked. She'd been thinking of something to say, and now she'd found the perfect question.

Victor's eyes widened. 'You may well ask.' Nervous suddenly, he glanced out of the window.

'Oh, Dad!' Jake gasped. He was staring down at Victor's car.

Victor moved towards him. 'I know.' Tess tried to squeeze between them. The car, sleek and long, blue over special blue, had been attacked. There were long white scratches and balloons of terrible words. One tyre had been punctured and lay like a puddle in the road.

'She's a werewolf.' Victor rested one hand on Jake's shoulder. 'At full moon she literally begins to howl.'

'Who?' Tess asked.

Just then there was a sharp ring on the bell.

Tess jumped and Jake, alarmed, leaped back from the window. But the ring was followed by some kind of code. Three short rings and then a longer, gentler ring like a call.

Victor calmly walked down to the door. It wasn't Georgina. There was a mumbling, a murmuring, a sort of coo, and Victor reappeared followed by a girl. She was young with short pale hair and she smiled shyly at Tess.

'This is Min,' Victor said, and he kicked her lovingly with the soft toe of his shoe.

'Hi.' Tess wondered if Min knew about them, about Georgina, the blue car and the moon.

'How long are you two here for?' Victor asked.

'Just for the day.'

Victor looked as if the day were rather a long time. He frowned and glanced around as if he'd noticed for the first time there was nowhere much to sit. 'Shall we go for lunch?'

Jake and Tess grinned with relief. 'Yes, please,' they said.

They walked back up to the Harrow Road and hailed a taxi. Victor sat on one of the flip-up chairs and faced them, one on either side of Min as they rattled through London. Occasionally he nuzzled Min's ankle with his toe. Min didn't respond. 'Where are we going?' she asked.

'What do you feel like?'

'Pie and Mash.'

'Waterloo,' Victor told the driver, who swerved in a U turn and drove the other way.

When they arrived Victor slipped into a phone box. Tess wondered if Min realized her jumper was on inside out. She'd look just right in the country, Tess thought, remembering Georgina and her coat.

The pie-and-mash shop was disgusting. There were eels and a green sauce to pour over the mash. Liquor, it was called.

Min only ate the eels and the inside of a pie. Jake, who even before William had been a vegetarian, just ate the mash.

'I've asked one of your sisters to come and join us,' Victor said, a wedge of eel grey between his teeth.

Tess tried to understand. She didn't like to argue but there were no sisters. Jake looked up as if the comment might have been for Min. 'I see,' he said when it was clear it wasn't.

'Where is she, anyway?' Victor glanced into the street and sighed.

They had almost finished and were getting ready to leave when Caro appeared. She was tall and broad and her hair was tied up in a scarf. She shook hands like a man.

'I'm starving,' she said and she ordered pie and mash, liquor and a huge mug of tea.

Caro had the longest eyelashes. They were curled and bright blue and each time she looked up they brushed the smooth arch of her brow. For a moment all four of them watched, entranced, as she ate.

'Roll up, roll up! The show's about to begin,' she laughed when she noticed and she cut a hole in her pie and let out a stream of sauce.

'How's college?' Min asked her. 'I haven't been in lately.'

'I noticed.' Caro narrowed her eyes. 'I told them you were sick.'

Victor smiled. 'I'll send a note.' Caro laughed but Min kicked him under the table so hard he winced. 'Or not.' He tried hard to catch her eye.

Tess lifted her fork to take another bite and remembered she didn't want any. Since William had decided they should all be vegetarian she couldn't imagine how she'd ever managed to eat meat.

'This pie is delicious,' Caro beamed and she caught Jake's eye. 'Want a bite?' She speared a huge chunk with her fork and, smiling right into his eyes, she aeroplaned it in.

Tess tweaked his arm. But Jake was still staring at Caro. 'It's good,' he said and he opened his mouth for more.

'We're carnivores in our family.' Caro nodded towards Dad. 'You know, he sometimes has lamb chops for breakfast. Lamb chops, rare steak.' She laughed. 'Me, I prefer kidneys on toast.'

Victor and Min were arguing. Their heads were close together and it was impossible to hear what they had to say. Min hissed out her words through gritted teeth. Even her eyes were closed.

'No brothers,' Caro was saying to Jake. 'Well, except you.' She opened her pearly mouth and laughed. 'Three

120

sisters. I'm the eldest. It's a bloody nightmare at home so I moved out.'

'Brilliant!' said Jake. 'That's just – '

'My Mum's not too bad, but there's this guy.'

'Yeah, we've got one of those.'

'He ordered a Lotus Europa through the post and now he's building it in what used to be our sitting room.'

'Our one's building a garage . . .'

'He never talks to us, or our Mum. He just spends all day on the phone swearing at the manufacturers, insisting that he's tried it every way, but the gearbox just won't fit in.'

'You've got a phone?'

'He put the telly in their bedroom, so you've got to step over his old undies if you want to switch it on.'

'A telly?'

'I gave it all up to have a bit of peace and quiet. I've got a bedsit in the Elephant and Castle. How old are you?'

Jake sat up in his chair. 'Twelve. Well, I will be in June.'

'I'm nine,' Tess said. 'Is there – is there anyone else my age, of your sisters?'

Caro thought for a moment. 'Yes. Bettina. She's ten. But she's not from Dad. You know.'

'I see,' said Tess. For a moment she'd had her and now she was gone.

'It's just me,' said Caro. 'In our family.'

Just Caro, thought Tess, and she was already Jake's.

'No, no, no, no. Ouch.' It was Min. Victor had his hand

around her neck. But now Min was laughing. She tusselled herself against him and for a moment they were still.

'Maybe sometime if I'm in London I could visit you?' Jake was eyeing Caro, watching her spooning in her pie.

'Yes.' She took a thirsty gulp of tea. 'Yes, except I'm thinking of going over to France to shack up with my boyfriend. He doesn't speak much English. He's great.' She slid Jake's plate towards her and, still hungry, finished up the cold remainder of his pie. 'If I come back I'll let you know.'

'Shhh now.' William pressed his hands together. There was a rare moment of silence as everyone bowed their heads. Usually he chose one of the children to say grace. He liked deliberating over which one he would pick as they sat, restless, anxious even, over their cooling food. But tonight it seemed appropriate that he should bless the meal himself. He'd made a vegetable pie and served it up on to octagonal red plates. They were the plates he'd brought from Italy on his honeymoon. Baked-earth plates from a market in Verona. But they were his plates, and he'd packed them in thick layers of newspaper so that not a single one was damaged in the move.

'We've got some news for you all.' He looked around the table and saw that Jake had noticed the pressure in his voice. He caught his eye and looked hard at him for a moment.

'Yes,' he said, turning towards Tess. 'Your Mummy and I, we've got some news.'

Francine was smiling. She hadn't stopped weeping and smiling for a week.

'Francine,' he said, as if translating for his daughters, 'is going to have a baby!' He smiled as well now, and the smile stuck in hard lines up by his eyes.

There was a pause as all five children looked at him, all five of them with their heads tilted to one side.

'Really?' It was Tess, pushing back the bench, almost falling as she rushed to throw herself into her mother's lap. 'It's what I've always wanted.' She had a sweeping feeling that the baby would be hers. 'A baby.'

'Hurray!' Sandy stood up on her bench. 'Hurrah!' Honour and Doon plinked their glasses with their spoons.

Jake cut through the noise. 'Haven't you heard of johnnies? You know, rubber johnnies and the Pill?'

Francine closed her eyes. She was pale now, the worry and dark shadows showing through. 'It was an accident,' she said, and her eyes spilled over with tears. Tess held her arms around her mother's neck and looked into her face. Even when she was crying she was still the most beautiful woman in the world.

'A happy accident.' William levelled her from the far end of the table. 'A happy accident, Francine.'

'A love child,' Doon giggled.

'A sexy yoni,' Sandy smirked.

'Come on, come on,' William laughed. 'Eat up before the food gets cold.' And there was a great cutting and mashing of pastry, chewing and exclaiming over how good it was.

'Where's the meat?' Jake asked. 'What are these? Some kind of beans?'

'Jake,' Tess hissed, 'don't ruin everything.' But in disgust Jake pushed away his plate.

William's eyes went black, and although he smiled, even Jake was too afraid to get down from the table until they were dismissed.

'I suppose the poor baby will be put on his pathetic rota,' Jake whispered as he slipped out of the room. 'Purple, red, blue, green . . .' he looked at Tess, 'and brown.'

Tess wanted to tell Mr Paul about the baby. She wanted to tell him how she was going to have her own baby sister or brother at last, but she was late arriving, they'd had to push start William's van, and Mr Paul had already plunged into his story. It was the story of Fenrir, one of Loki's bastard children, and how as a trick the gods bound him with a chain. Fenrir didn't want to be bound by a chain as smooth as a silk ribbon fashioned especially by dwarfs, but then he didn't want to be accused of cowardice. So before agreeing to be bound, as an act of faith Fenrir ordered one of the gods to put his hand into his mouth.

If Fenrir couldn't escape from this chain, as he had from all the others, then he would gnash his teeth together and the god would lose his hand.

'What was the chain made from? Does anybody know?' Mr Paul leant towards them. 'The sound a cat makes when it moves.' He answered his own question. 'A woman's beard. The roots of a mountain. The sinews of a bear.'

But Tess was waiting to know what happened to Fenrir. She clutched her own hand tight around the wrist and tried to see what Mr Paul had drawn for them on the next board.

'The breath of a fish, and a bird's spittle,' he finished and with a sweep he rolled up the board. Fenrir could never escape from a chain made from so many magic things, and there was the wolf with a hand like a tongue hanging from his mouth. His fangs were huge and yellow and blood dripped in crimson chalk. A murmur of disgust rose up from the children. Delicious, delighted groans.

'The gods fastened the chain through the hole of a huge boulder, looped it back on itself and drove the boulder a mile down into the earth.' Mr Paul's eyes shone with success. 'Fenrir shook and wrestled. He grated his teeth and opened his bloodstained jaws. Then one of the gods drew his sword. He drove the point hard into the roof of Fenrir's mouth and rammed the hilt against his lower jaw. The wolf was gagged. His howls were terrible and slaver streamed from his jaws.' Mr Paul stood still in the centre of the room. 'And so, gagged and bound, Fenrir can do nothing but wait for Ragnarok.'

'Jake. What is Ragnarok?'

Jake wasn't listening.

'Will it be very terrible?'

Jake sighed with irritation. 'It's the battle to end all battles and when it comes the world will end.'

'But when will it be?'

Jake winked and smiled. He put a holy lilt into his voice. 'That is something no one knows.'

'Not even Mr Paul?'

Jake went back to his letter. 'How do you spell dear?'

'Like the animal?'

'No stupid, like Dear Cyril Littlewood.'

'Maybe the baby could be called Cyril, I mean if it's a boy.'

'Dear Cyril Littlewood, I wonder if I could come and work permanently with you as a volunteer. I'm strong, I can cut logs with a chainsaw, sail a boat and I even know something about bricklaying.'

Tess watched him. 'You see.'

'What?' Jake looked up, his face was flushed with hope and the hard, hard work of spelling.

'You're getting to be like him. Like William.'

Jake's shoulders hunched. He screwed the letter into a ball and threw it across the floor. 'Don't be disgusting.'

He started a clean page. 'Dear Cyril Littlewood. I need a job. I can write stories for you about animals in f– How do you spell foreign?'

But before Tess could tell him he'd slumped over in despair. 'Anyway,' he said, 'it's bound to be a girl.'

As spring opened into summer William flew into a flurry of activity. He built the chicken coop, cleared a whole stretch of the wild and brought home two bantam hens and a cock.

'I wonder,' he said, examining the faces round the table, 'who could take on the task of caring for the chickens?'

'No!' Tess waved her arms so urgently she knocked over a glass. 'It's me, it's my job, you promised it when we first moved in.'

'All right, calm down.' He tried to smile. He'd been looking forward to handing out this chore, taking it apart in little portions. 'Well, if you're going to do the job, you'll have to do it all. They'll need feeding twice a day, locking up at night if you don't want the fox to get them, and at weekends their hutch will have to be mucked out.'

'Who'll collect the eggs?' Doon asked.

William paused and the whole table waited with him. 'I thought we should let them sit. Bantams are good sitters. They can hatch out chicks and we'll build up a little flock.'

Francine smiled warmly at him. There was an air of

conspiracy about her now, and it still surprised him when quite openly she walked up the stairs and settled herself in his room.

Henrietta, the brightest, brownest hen, was chosen to do the sitting. She wasn't allowed to sit on her own eggs but on a clutch of three speckled Marrons William brought back from the biodynamic farm. Marron hens were better layers, bigger, stronger birds, and instead of her own chicks Henrietta was going to hatch the Marrons out. Tess felt a little sorry for her, her tiny, neat brown body settled round those outsized eggs while her sister Rebecca and Chanticleer the cock pecked and strutted and explored the boundaries of the wild.

'I wonder if we'll still have to pay rent?' Jake said. 'Now that Mum's . . . you know,' his voice hushed to an ominous whisper, 'gone upstairs.'

'Pay rent?' Had they been paying rent? It seemed strange that William should need more money when there was a badminton net and enough money on Saturdays to hire a boat. But William had explained quite often that really they were poor. They were the workers. The real people of the land. Teachers and cooks and gardeners. He winked at Francine when he mentioned gardening, because now that she was having a baby she'd had to give up her teacher-training course. It made her sick, the smell of the corridors, and she only wanted to be in the fresh

128

air. And then there was maintenance for Felicity. William's face froze when he spoke of this. 'When really she should be paying me.'

'If there is a revolution,' he told them, 'we'll be with the rebels.' He raised his arm in a powerful Red Army salute. Tess shook her fist and laughed. She imagined revolutionaries swarming over the cattle grid, the thick dark leaves of rhododendrons brushing against their coats.

'But how will they know?' she'd asked. 'How will they know we're rebels?' She could see them stop to shoot the Darlbys in the coachhouse, raise their bayonets to Peter and Prue who lived with a Retriever in a flat above the stables, but when they got to The Wild, with its garage and conservatory how would they know that their house was on the Revolution's side?

'I don't think we'll have to pay rent,' she said to Jake, 'because that's why we're getting a lodger.'

'Yes,' Jake mused. 'Maybe the whole baby thing was a plan to free up an extra room.'

Tess didn't reply.

'More money for Pale Face. You know he's saving up to sail off to the North Pole? To see if it's really colder there than the Ashdown Forest Reservoir.'

Tess climbed into bed and curled into a ball. Her plastic sheet creaked and ridged under her side. It had been seven days since . . . her chest contracted with the fear of counting, and then a quick spark of elation lit up in her head. Maybe it's over. Maybe it's all in the past. Yes, I used to wet my bed, but now . . . now that I'm ten, oh not for a long time now.

'What I don't understand,' Jake was talking through the mattress, 'is why even the lodger has to be a girl.'

The lodger was American, big boned, with pale red frizzy hair, and she'd been rescued from a cult. It was a cult where everybody wore white and the luckiest and prettiest of the women, the Hand Maidens, were allowed to drive around in the Leader's white Rolls-Royce. The lodger's real name was Melody, but in the cult she'd been renamed Perpetual Love.

Melody was seventeen and she was going into the last term of Class Eleven. 'How did you get away?' Tess and Doon watched her with wide admiring eyes. 'How did you escape?' They followed her through into her room, and clambered up on to Francine's abandoned bed.

'I didn't get away.' Melody spoke with slow American vowels. 'I was kidnapped.'

Tess and Doon gasped. 'Who by?'

Melody hunched her shoulders. 'My Mom.'

'Does that mean you want to go back?' They were appalled.

'I'll go back some day.' She fixed them with the huge experience of her eyes. 'When I've done my A-levels.'

The children weren't supposed to know about the cult,

130

but Jake had overheard William discussing it as he sat in the fireplace, tuning his guitar for songs. 'She's at a very impressionable age,' he'd told Francine. 'She needs to be sheltered for a while from the world. Perpetual Love, I ask you.' William had snorted. 'I bet Big Daddy called all the girls that.'

'Maybe we could rename Spotless Perpetual Love,' Jake suggested as they took him for a walk up on to the golf-course.

'Perpetual Love.' Honour blushed scarlet as she said it, and the stick she threw caught up in a tree. 'Perpetual!' she called, but the dog, instead of running back, twisted in a wild dance, scampering in and out of bracken until Honour sternly called out 'Spotless!' and he came lolloping back.

Jake pulled out his penknife and cut himself a stick. 'Onward march,' he ordered and he led the four girls up on to the top green of the golf-course, where they could look right down over the land. There were stretches of wild grass, birch trees and silver larch, pale shoots of bracken furling out of brown, and in a little dip, the island of the Jenkinshaws' small house. They could even see Mr Jenkinshaw bent over in his garden, pulling up the weeds between the rows of sprouts. They could hear the chiming of the church clock at Twelve Ashes and see the thin spire sticking up above a clump of trees. Jake took off his shoes and socks and pressed his feet into the green green grass. It was cool and springy, clipped and watered to a sheen, and when you ran your hand across it, it was like touching someone's newly scissored hair. Jake lay on his side and, denting in the imprint of his body, stretched out his arms and rolled. Tess pulled off her own shoes and rolled too. The ground was springy as a bed and as she rolled small husks and twists of grass tickled in her nose.

'Look at me!' Sandy shouted and she threw herself into a cartwheel so vigorously that her feet flipped over into a crab. In the distance golfers toiled towards them, gorse yellow in their patterned clothes.

'Let's look for golf balls,' Doon suggested, the glint of money in her eyes.

But Jake laughed, sticking out his tongue. 'I know.' He leapt up and, running back across the green, pulled out the flag and threw it javelin style into the grass. 'Help me,' he called to the others, and in a sudden rush they began scrabbling for twigs and bracken, anything to cover up the pole. 'They'll be wandering about all afternoon like sheep looking for the eighteenth hole,' Jake laughed and he stood up to watch two small burdened figures already veering off the other way.

'We are the red men, feathers-in-our-head men, down upon the dead men. Pow wow.' The children raced down the hill, up mounds, along lanes, breathing in the damp sweet dewy smell of spring. The first cut grass, the narrow silver trees, the tops of bracken like caterpillars unfurling into green.

'Let's never go back, never go back.' Jake stretched his arms.

But when the sun began to drift behind the hills and the grass turned cool, Sandy started to wilt. 'I'm hungry,' she said.

'Eat berries,' Jake told her, but Doon was worried her guinea-pigs wouldn't know where she'd gone and she wanted to go home too.

'Come on.' Honour gathered her sisters to her. 'Spot-less, come here. Home.' She looked at Tess, picking burs out of her hair.

'I'm hungry as well, Jake,' Tess said, letting him decide, and she waited for him to push on past her, beating the hedgerows with a stick, so she could follow along behind.

William was proud to be the one to keep an eye on Melody. Proud to have been chosen for the job. Melody needed someone stable, someone firm, someone with a talent to really understand the young. He pulled on his tightest trousers and a jacket with a smart patch on the arm and as an extravagant treat he drove into East Grinstead and bought three different kinds of cheese, white wine and a French loaf to dip into fondue.

'I'm macrobiotic,' Melody said as the children knelt up on their benches to dip small squares of bread into the melting cheese.

William swallowed. 'Macro–?' Of course he knew what she meant, he just couldn't quite recollect the details.

'Macrobiotic is a way of eating in tune with nature, using only the vegetables and fruit in season.' She glanced at the soft white squares of bread. 'I only eat wholegrain flour.'

'Oh.' William looked quite genuinely sad. 'Usually everything we eat here is grown in the garden. We have our own potatoes, onions, carrots, spinach. Soon we'll have our own eggs.'

'Eggs are out,' Melody said.

'We're only having fondue,' William's voice dropped almost to a whine, 'as a sort of rather special treat.'

Jake paused with a long rubbery string of cheese hanging from his fork. He glanced up at William and saw he'd gone into a sulk.

'He'll feel sorry for him now,' Tess hoped, but Jake's smile rolled up into a smirk.

Henrietta hatched out her eggs in the middle of June. Three tiny fluffy chicks. Tess rushed in at breakfast time to give the news. 'They've hatched! They've hatched!' She was spluttering with excitement.

William had his hands pressed together in prayer.

'Before the flour the mill,
Before the mill the grain,

Before the grain, the sun, the earth, the rain,
The beauty of God's will.'

'Now,' William turned to her and she felt herself swell with his attention. 'Every good poultrywoman keeps a record of the development of their fowl.' He handed her a tiny notebook with a pen in a plastic loop across the top. 'A daily record,' he told her, and in silence he spooned muesli into his mouth.

Day one, Tess wrote, *Chicks hatched.*
Day two. Chicks doing well.
Day three. Chicks eating well.

After a week even Tess could see that it was boring, but diligently she went on. *Chicks doing well. Chicks still doing well. Chicks pecking corn from hand.*

The chicks were going to be hens, at least as far as anyone could tell, and for several days the conversation about what they should be called took over from the list of names being collected for the baby. Moses, Joshua, Pip, Skye, Mordecai, Rupert. Half the page was supposed to be for girls but it was so full of blanks and spaces that soon Thomas, Elias and Orlando had burst over from the other side. The baby page was pinned up behind the kitchen door, just above the rota, and when no one was in the kitchen Jake used it as a dartboard. He screwed up one eye and threw the darts with such precision that soon each name was snagged with tears. 'Don't do that,' Tess begged. But Jake threw one dart so hard that Moses disappeared into a hole.

Chicks eating well and healthy.
Chicks hopped down the ramp.
Chicks hopped up the ramp!

Dear Dad,
The littlest chick has broken its leg. William thinks it will survive. It stands on one leg and makes a sort of peeping noise. It can hop down the ramp but I have to carry it back to its nest. I'm calling it Eliza. Mum was a bit upset because she was saving that name for the baby in case it's a girl. Did you know she was having a baby? Anyway, if it's a girl she can have Eliza back and the chick can be called Esmerelda. How's ~~Geor~~ How's Min? Odin is very well. I wish you could see him jump out of the vegetables and catch birds. He just swipes them out of the air and then he tears their heads off. The other day I found a claw and a beak on the floor of my room.
Love Tess

Jake had been chosen to say Grace. 'I'll make a fuss of him,' William decided. 'That's all he needs.' He poured milk over his muesli as he looked through his post. Bills, and the red reminders for bills, and one tantalizing envelope, rich and creamy with an elegant curved edge. He sliced it open with his knife.

'You're a first class wanker with a pocketful of fish.'

William felt himself go white. His hands trembled as he turned the letter over to scrutinize the form of the address, the inky 'Wild' underlined, and the London postmark stamped across the pale-green queen.

'For what we are about to receive may the Lord make us truly grateful,' Jake mumbled.

'Anything interesting?' Francine met his eye as he looked up, and he smiled and shook his head, slipping the letter back into its envelope and pushing it under his bowl.

'So, Jake,' William continued steadfast with his plan, 'what have you got today?'

'Games, metalwork, painting, the usual sorts of things.' Jake fixed him with a stare of such ferocity that out of sheer confusion William cupped his hand over his deaf car. 'Games, did you say? What's Mr Bindley doing with you this term?'

'Well it's hardly likely he's entered us for the county football championships.'

William looked down at his muesli and attempted to laugh.

'Why's no one at George House allowed to play foot-ball?' Doon asked.

'What is football?' Sandy dropped her spoon and

had to climb under the table to wrestle it away from the dog.

'Football,' William crossed his arms, 'is a highly aggressive sport. Feet are for walking and running. If you're encouraged to use your feet to kick, to kick balls, then soon it will be another kind of balls you'll be kicking.' William smirked and the girls, unsure quite why he was laughing, laughed too.

'Ha ha bollocks,' Jake said, and Francine tried to hide her smile.

'Jake,' William was determined to draw the conversation back, 'I've been thinking about your music lessons. Maybe you should consider taking up the violin like Honour?'

'Yes,' Jake said. 'But I'd prefer to play the trumpet.'

'Of course,' William said, and he cradled his deaf ear.

'He'll have to put his hand in his pocket for the lessons,' Jake leant down to Tess, 'if he can fit it in there with his trousers so tight.'

'Yes.' Tess was thinking about the night before, how she'd woken, walked through the cold dark hall, sat on the black plastic seat of the toilet and felt the tingling water stream into the bowl. It had splashed hotly on her legs, the last drops sliding against porcelain, and then she'd woken to find herself lying on her own wet stinking bed. She closed her eyes and prayed. 'Please please please

God . . .' but she was walking on a top-heavy cliff, and the hair-line cracks were opening. They were widening into gulfs, cracking just under her toes until she was stranded on one narrow, snaking ridge. 'I'll fall, I'll fall,' she fought against her pillow and suddenly she dropped like a stone into sleep.

When Tess got back from school she found her father in the kitchen. He wasn't wearing his smart suit, but looked all rumpled as if he'd driven straight to Sussex from his bed. She crept through the front door and stood against the wall.

'It's ridiculous, you can't go through with it,' Victor was saying. His hands were clenched around the Rayburn's rail, his face a hot reflection in the oblong hood.

Tess heard her mother's incredulous gasp.

'He's a fake,' said Victor.

Tess stood silent, not wanting them to know she'd overheard.

'A fanatic and a fake.'

'You don't know him.' Francine shook her head and she turned her back on Victor to grate a huge yellow pyramid of cheese.

Tess sidled a little further into the room. Her mother already looked bulky from behind, the baby pushing out the slim line of her waist, denting small fat ripples into the waistband of her skirt.

'If there was only something I could do.' Victor's voice was mournful.

'Well,' Francine smiled, but her eyes were faraway and cold, 'you could pay for Jake's music lessons. Did you know he's going to learn the trumpet?'

'For God's sake. The boy can't even spell. Trumpet. What's the point of that?'

There was a long silence in which Tess wondered if she could ease herself outside and start again.

'You see, what I don't understand,' Victor said eventually, 'is why make all the effort to get out of medieval times if you're going to pretend you're still in them.' He put his hands in his pockets and moved towards the kitchen door.

'You're not staying?'

'I'd better get back. Will you give this to the children?' Tess pressed herself against the wall and as she did so she heard the slide and crackle of new notes.

Dear Dad,
The Gods of the Norse Myths do such disgusting things. Especially Loki who cut off Syf's hair and then as a punishment the dwarves sewed up his mouth. He just ripped the stitches out, can you imagine? Jake's playing the trumpet. He practises in the kitchen and whenever he starts William goes out to mend the van.
Love Tess

★

William needed to keep busy. He built an extra floor above the garage and hired men to help him put on the roof. This room would be a workshop for the children. He screwed trapeze bars into the ceiling and clipped up a swing. He brought home a huge slab of clay wrapped for moisture in a plastic sheet, and he laid out boards for rolling, cutting and sculpting. 'They can model, carve, sculpt, swing, sing, play dolls' houses.' Inside his head a small voice soothed, 'Anything, anything to get them out of the house.'

Francine watched him from the workshop door. 'What lucky children,' she smiled. William glanced up at her leaning, smiling in the sun, and he broke out in a sweat. Another baby. He planed a long soft curve of pine. Small curls of warm white wood rolled on to the floor.

'But William?' For a long second he thought she'd gone away. 'But William, it is Sunday . . .' Francine was trying to draw him towards her with her eyes. 'Couldn't you take a break?'

'Yes,' he said, but he went on planing. He was making the wooden base for a bed to knock up in the corner. More space, more beds, more people. He had to get it done.

She stood in the doorway and smoothed her hand over the just visible bulge. Her cheeks were rosy and her eyes glowed with a new shine. 'I thought we could take the van and go off for a drive. Or even walk up on to the golf-course, just on our own.'

'Yes,' he said, 'of course, I'll be right with you.' But he didn't stop.

Honour, Doon and Sandy were going to Scotland as soon as the summer term broke up. William was going to drive them, and because of that he had to take the entire engine of the van apart and see if he could mend it. He opened up the other bonnet and kept it open so he could rifle through the engine for spare parts.

He was so busy, so bent over the prongs and twirls of the twin engines, that he didn't notice Honour when she came home with brand-new eyes. She sat down for supper, all shy and grinning, her glasses folded neatly away inside their case. 'Daddy,' she said once he'd scrubbed his hands with Swarfega, 'Daddy,' but instead of her he looked around the table, at the six bent heads of female hair, all long and trailing except for Melody's fiery frizz of ginger curls.

'Miss Glot says I don't have to wear them any more.' Honour looked up at him, and as if for the first time he saw the gold flecks in her eyes, gold flecks instead of glass.

'Mummy won't recognize you,' Doon said.

'Shhh,' William frowned, but not before a look of terror had shot across Honour's face.

Doon bit her lip. 'I'm sorry.' But Honour had already slipped down from the table, tramped up the stairs and was lying with the sheet over her head.

William closed his eyes but instead of sleep he saw the endless gulf of sky that stretched away on every side from Cammothmore. It was still his village, still his name on the deeds of the house, and his money paid half the bills. But it wasn't what he'd wanted. That wide open landscape, cold winds and heather, and the weed smell of the sea. It was the place his father had been formed by, stark and rough and wild, and to his surprise, after forcing her to move there, it was Felicity who took it to her heart. She fell instantly in love with it, the tufted grass, the way it grew all heathery right up to the windows, and sometimes she lay down on the rough beds of their garden and stretched her arms out to the sky. It had unsettled him, the silence of it, and the way Felicity could see him, several miles away, as he drove down the long straight lane from work.

'I'm o'er young, I'm o'er young, I'm o'er young to marry yet;
I'm o'er young, 'twad be a sin . . .'

He recited Burns to help him sleep, knowing all the time it was quite useless. Eventually he got up and wandered about the house. He could hear the night-time noises, the whirr of the boiler and the drip of a faulty downstairs tap. The occasional rumble of a car, splashing on the road outside. He pushed open the door and stepped into the garden. The hens were locked into their shed, the guinea-pigs, all eleven of them, were safely in their hutches. Even Spotless, meek in sleep, was curled against the Rayburn's wall. 'I'm o'er young,' he smiled, glancing up at the stars, and then Odin leapt up against the window of Jake's room and hissed at him through the glass. William almost shouted out with fright. Bastard. He shook his fist. Bastard, and when he'd taken control of himself he mouthed, 'Cat soup,' although he knew it was stupid to be so riled by a cat. Odin smiled his orange smile and curled his tail as he walked back along the window-sill.

'Mummy! Mummy! Mummy!' The rule against Felicity had broken free. The Strachan girls were going back to Scotland, to the house where they'd been born. For the first time they were going to see their brother.

William's face was black with grease and oil. 'Will you stay there long?' Francine asked him, and he tightened a bolt and said he'd drop them off and turn right round.

'Well you can't just drive straight back. It's hundreds of miles.'

William pushed his sleeve up over his arm and flexed a muscle. 'I can,' he said, and then conceded he'd have to stay one night. 'I'll sleep in the van. I'll park it as far from the house as I can get.'

Henrietta very happy and chicks very fat.
Chick with broken leg puts its leg on ground sometimes.

Henrietta doesn't sleep with chicks any more.
Chicks fly off ramp.

The Wild wasn't the same without the Strachans. So quiet and still. Tess wandered round the house, staring guiltily into the deserted rooms. She flicked through the books by Honour's bed and chose a mandarin's outfit from Doon and Sandy's dressing-up box. She tiptoed up to Melody's door and stood there listening to see if she had gone. 'Come in Tess,' Melody called wearily. Embarrassed, Tess pushed open the door. 'You'd make a lousy detective, I could probably hear you breathing from LA.'

Melody was packing. Tess checked to see how many of her clothes were white. 'What if you never come back?'

'I'll be back.' In a separate bag she had packed a whole brown-pastry pie she'd made herself.

'But if you don't come back, shall we come and rescue you?'

'Don't worry.' Melody smiled. 'After all, who needs Big Daddy when you've got Wild Willy at home?'

Tess didn't know what she meant. But she did know William didn't like to be called Willy. Will or Bill got on his nerves. Jake tried sometimes casually to slip in Billy, but the dark blood that flooded through William's face warned him to stop. 'Wooden Will,' Jake whispered just under his breath, but he took care to move round to his deaf side.

★

Jake cooked a celebration cheese on toast. Two slices each with vinegar and extra cheese. It was harder to cook it without a grill and he had to put it in the oven of the Rayburn on a tray. 'Supper's ready,' he called, although Tess and Francine were waiting. The table looked vast and empty and Tess slithered along the bench to make less room.

'For what we are about to receive may the Lord make us truly fartful.' Jake was solemn, and he looked up at Francine to catch her smile.

'I think I'll sit here.' Jake took his plate and moved over to William's chair. 'Oh yes, this is perfect.' He put down his knife and fork and, smiling gleefully, he ate his supper with his hands.

First thing in the morning, Tess let the chickens out, put the guinea-pigs in their run, and went with Jake up on to the forest. The earth was sweet and spongy and all across the grass daisies in white sweeps were folding back the pink undersides of petals. Spotless leapt and bounded and dug small holes in the greens.

'Spotless!' Tess scowled, but Jake laughed and urged him on.

'Let's make a camp and stay up here all day.' Jake pulled out a small axe like a tomahawk and hacked down a bush. He tilted it against another, overlapping the branches to make a tent. He padded the gaps between with bracken.

'We need dry grass for a carpet,' he ordered, and Tess wandered between the bushes pulling up great armfuls of pale dry hay. She pushed it into the camp in rolls and when it wouldn't sink she trampled it flat with her feet. When the carpet was ready they crawled into the cool, green shadow of the camp and lay back on the hay. 'I'm Chief Wise Eagle,' Jake said, 'and you can be my squaw.'

Tess squinted at the filtered streaks of sky, and sang.

'In olden times there was a river,
Flowed between two mountain walls,
And the people in that valley
Called that place the haunted falls.'

'That's a white man's song, silly,' Jake said, but the tune was too mesmeric to let go.

'They pulled a mother from her children,
Paid no heed to their piteous cries,
Threw her on the rocks beneath them,
Where in agony she died.'

Together they joined in the gruesome chorus, imagining themselves the first settlers in a hostile land.

'If 'twas revenge that they were after,
'Twas revenge that they did find,

When they killed those little babies
And burned the cabin to the ground.'

'Shhhh.' Jake craned his neck out of the camp. Two golfers in short-sleeved patterned shirts were ambling past.

'My God, where's Spotless?' Tess crawled out on her hands and knees. Spotless was lying on the carpet of the green, his legs stretched out in heaven, sleeping with his back against the flag. Beside him, like a line of mole hills, small hillocks of dried earth were heaped where he'd been searching for a bone.

Jake put his fingers in his mouth and whistled, and even before the golfers had a chance to aim, Spotless was rushing towards them. They abandoned their camp and ran, leaping ditches and scratching through long grass, laughing at the angry shouts that floated after them, stumbling and gasping until they reached the lane that led up beside the shop.

Out of habit Jake stopped at the phone box. He pulled open the heavy door and dialled. The phone rang for a long time but there was no reply.

Tess took her mainlesson book up on to the golf-course while Jake built them a new camp. Her summer project was to illustrate the story of Thor's Hammer. Mr Paul had told it to them on the last day of term and as a treat he'd taken them into the valley field, and sat with them in a circle on the grass.

Tess prised open her Caran d'Ache, the flat metal buckling as she unclicked the catch so that pencils sprayed out into the grass. She picked them up and arranged them in their order in the box, rippling them in their individual grooves to watch the colours spin. She chose a green for Thrym. Thrym was the frost giant who wanted to marry Freya and because of this Thor had smashed his hammer into his skull. Poor Thrym. She wanted to show him startled, jumping back in fear when the bridal veil was lifted and he saw, instead of Freya, Thor's coal-red eyes. Tess chose a green and then a grey, the colours, softened by the sun, smudging against the page.

Mr Paul, Mr Paul, she thought, where are you to help with Thrym? She needed his sure hand to make the hair. But Mr Paul was on holiday with his daughter. They had gone to Cornwall, and when they got back, Mr Paul was going to tell them all about the princesses, sorcerers, and the knights of the round table where Arthur sat. She gave the frost giant yellow and orange eyes and made his head reach almost to the sky. But then she remembered she had the whole long summer holidays to finish it and she'd better stop or there'd be nothing left to do. She stretched out on the warm dry grass and watched a golfer walking slowly nearer and then stopping to bend and swoop and practise his low swing.

*

After three days William still wasn't back. Jake sat in his seat and mumbled a rude prayer and Francine let them have toast and Marmite for their supper. Afterwards they stood up against the Rayburn and made caramel with brown sugar and butter in a pan.

'I'll have a piece.' Francine held out her hand, and Tess saw that even her wrist was beginning to get fat.

Jake sighed. 'Maybe none of them will ever come back.' He spread his arms wide as if to test out so much space.

'Jake, don't.' Francine swallowed and a film of tears slid across each eye. Then she looked up. 'We've been here a whole year.' For a second they all looked at each other startled, and then Jake said brightly, 'So I suppose it's time to move?'

'Odin.' Tess remembered the reason they'd been asked to move before, and she raced out into the garden where she found him watching the chickens menacingly from a tree. 'Odin!' He dropped down into her arms, folding his claws under especially for her. 'You like it here, don't you?' she asked, and when he closed his orange eyes and rubbed his chin against her face she knew it meant he did.

When Jake had first got Odin they'd been living with a family in a house opposite the school. The family was divorcing, and the wife wanted other people there so she didn't notice the emptiness so much. There was one unusually pretty little girl, and a garden with snapdragons, and convolvulus winding in the hedge. For a moment it looked as if they'd found a place to stay. But then miserably the wife discovered she was pregnant, and in the chaos and confusion Francine thought it best if they, and not the husband, moved away. For several months they'd lived in two beige rooms above a food shop, but then the owner accused Jake of stealing tinned spaghetti hoops and using his old screwdriver to get into the tins. 'He never would,' Francine sprang to his defence. 'He doesn't even know what tinned spaghetti is.' But they still had to go.

The next place they lived was a council house up on the hill above Twelve Ashes. The houses were square and low and the one they lived in they shared with a man of eighty-two. His bath was in the kitchen and the toilet was outside in a spidery plank-board shed. The planks were full of knots and eyes and Jake poked every one of them until one popped out and left a hole. At first it was quite nice to glimpse the garden as you sat on the cold seat, but when the winter came a sharp wind whistled through at you, chilling your bare bottom as you pulled down your clothes to pee. The old man, Mr Parish, needed someone to bring him cups of tea and keep an eye on him if he nodded off with his gas fire on, but one night when Francine came home late she found the door was bolted against her from inside. She knocked and called and then she threw a pebble at the window. 'Mr Parish,' she called, the children lolling half asleep against her side. 'Mr Parish! Open the door.'

'I will not.' His head appeared at the window, and he leant out and called her a dirty whore.

'We've only been to a barn dance.' Francine's first instinct was to laugh, and all the lights along the street went on.

'Barn dance, barn dance, my arse, you should leave those children home where they belong.'

Tess clutched at Francine's hand. She didn't want to be left at home with Mr Parish. Once he'd made her kiss him in exchange for an orange horseshoe made from glass. His cheek was flannelly and grooved. There were tiny bristles on it and it smelt of grey.

'Let me in this minute,' Francine demanded so sternly that he pulled back from the window, and soon they heard him fumbling on the stairs. 'I'm sorry,' he said, his pale-pink eyes blinking in the darkness. 'I'm sorry.' He tried to pluck at her clothes. But the next morning Francine packed up their possessions and moved on.

When William eventually arrived back from Cammoth-more he had a caravan trailing behind his van. It was an old gypsy caravan on wooden wheels with the paintwork worn and flaking off. 'A summer project,' he said, 'for Jake and Tess.' He pulled the caravan himself to the far end of the wild and parked it under the trees. 'I'm going to teach you two to restore this caravan, starting from scratch. What's this?' He pulled two sheets of sandpaper out as though they were sweets. 'Well done,' he beamed.

'Right, now we can get on. I'll help you a little, but you're going to do most of it yourselves.'

'Really?' Tess skipped and spun, as if the caravan really was a treat, while Jake flicked through the colour chart for shades to match the paint. It was clear the caravan had once been red and green, with flowers curled in orange just above the door.

'No, no, no.' William flipped at Jake's hand and snatched the charts away. 'Not for a long time, that's the last, last thing to be done. The final reward for preparation.'

Jake hung his head. He looked quite desperately dark.

'It's all right Jake,' Tess nudged him. 'Just think how lovely it will be when it's finished. We'll be able to play in there. Have tea parties and camps. It can be our camp for winter.' She was going to say she'd let him put his posters up on the green wooden walls when William interrupted.

'I'll be using it as my study, so we'll need to get it finished by the autumn term.' And he left them alone with the sandpaper.

William sat up at his desk and worked on the next year's curriculum. He wanted to move his class from the Ancient Greeks right through to modern times with the History of the Theatre. For Alison in particular he had high hopes. She was light and elegant and had moved through his modern version of *Oedipus* with a silken voice. If he could just engage her in the real intensity of the part she would flourish into life. If only she could live a little, experience some real pleasure and some pain.

Occasionally he looked out of the window. He could see the children sanding diligently away, while Francine rested on the caravan steps. 'They'll thank me.' He smiled as he looked down on their bent heads. 'When they come to putting shelves up or sanding floors, they'll thank me and not their father, who'll have nothing to advise them on except which brand of cigarettes to smoke.'

Francine had pulled on dungarees and was helping gouge old putty from the window frames. He could almost see the sweat break out on her face and he pushed the window open to waft some air into the room. He wanted to go out and join them, strip his shirt off and feel the wooden handles of the plane, smell the toxic smell of Nitromorse, and watch as it burst ripples through the paint. He could almost feel the satisfaction of sliding the flat-ended chisel against wood, but he had to sit at his desk and force himself into his work. He bit the low lip of his smile to think that Jake was too young for Nitromorse. It was too dangerous for a boy of twelve, and anyway he'd accepted the sandpaper. William could see him now, toiling away with the harshest grade, splinters of paint flicking up under his nails. 'He's young and strong, he'll manage.' He turned back to his papers and felt his own thin sweat soak rings into his shirt.

★

Tess and Jake worked on the caravan every morning and in the afternoons they went up on to the forest to their camp. Jake took his axe and swiped at the long grass. Sometimes they lingered round the phone box, marking dusty patterns on the glass, and once Jake wrote across three squares – WILLIAM IS A DIG PIG. Tess turned the DIG to BIG for him before they ran off to train Spotless to hate golf. 'Spotless! Spotless!' they called and they let him off the lead and watched him wriggle away into the bracken. They heard some growling followed by a frightened shriek and when they tramped through the undergrowth they came out by a green river of grass to find a caddy pinned up against a tree. The caddy was a boy about as tall as Jake.

'D'you get paid?' Jake asked him when they'd pulled Spotless off.

'Yes.' The boy began to breathe again and he showed them his hand, which had a small blue nip. 'It bit me, your dog. Someone should put it down.'

'Someone should put you down,' Jake snarled and they watched as the boy collected the rattling bag of clubs and pulled them up the hill to where a huge man in a short-sleeved shirt was waiting, his face dark red from the heat.

Dear Dad and Min,
We're having a really great summer. Painting a caravan. Jake's pulling out old nails and I'm sanding. If we ever

find ourselves stranded in the Revolution we'll be able to manage.

Love Tess

The next time they passed the phone box, the phone started to ring. Jake jumped and Tess felt the hairs prickle up along her neck. 'Dad!' They both turned and ran to get to it.

'Hello?' Jake's smile was as wide as a tree. 'Hello?' There was a pause in which his whole face frowned. 'No,' he said. There was another pause. 'Wrong number. Wrong number!' he screamed, and still holding the phone he hissed ice cold and clear, 'You silly fucking cow.'

'Jake.' Tess was frightened. She stroked his arm. 'Jake.' But all afternoon as they trailed through the forest, poking in the streams for golf balls and lying down to rest in small wild cuts of hay, he stayed far away from her and cold.

There was no one in the kitchen and the letter had been lying all morning, unnoticed on the mat. Tess picked it up. It was addressed to both of them, to her and Jake, and the lines of the address were in her father's hand. His writing was so perfect, so liquid clear and blue, it looked like a flower floating on a vine. Jake came in and knelt up against the table. Finally he'd been allowed the colour chart and he was spreading it over the wood. His hands were streaked with undercoat, his hair thick white with dust, but at last the wooden hull of the caravan was smooth and stripped and ready for the paint. 'What colours shall we choose?' Jake asked, a glint of pleasure creeping up into his eyes. 'Let's go into East Grinstead and choose.' He let his fingers trail over the rectangular shades.

William was standing at the door. 'There is one last thing to be done. How can you buy paint before you know how much paint you'll need?' He cocked his head to one side as if the idea of making calculations would somehow be fun. Tess folded her father's letter and pressed it into the pocket of her shorts. 'Right, who wants the tape measure?'

Tess and Jake measured every corner of the caravan, writing down their findings on the back of the colour chart. They subtracted the windows and added on the floor and then attempted to convert the numbers into paint. George House hadn't equipped them for such things. Square feet, fluid ounces, litres, gallons, pints. They weren't exactly sure what they were supposed to find.

'Where's Mum?' Tess asked, not because she thought she would be helpful, but simply to stop the endless adding up.

'She's, you know . . .' Jake sighed. Francine had gone off to the hospital. The baby wasn't due for four and a half months, but everyone wanted to know why she was getting so big. 'Perhaps it's twins?' Tess had suggested and both Jake and William had jerked upright, their faces white. Francine's wrists were thick, her fingers fattened and her feet had grown too wide for any shoes. She walked around in wellingtons, sloshing through the grass, and when it was too hot she swung them off and let her swollen toes sink into the earth.

'What have you come up with?' William startled them as he strode out of the trees.

'1.8 litres and another 3.75 for the outside.' Jake made a random guess, screwing their maths into a ball.

In the hardware shop William breathed in the sandpaper air. There was the oil-hot smell of screws, chains, cut keys, and the eggshell cloy of paint. He'd forgotten about Jake's maths, which was a disgrace, and the fact that Tess didn't even know how to turn twelve inches into a square foot. 'I'll have two large tins of green,' he ordered. 'And a small tin of orange.' That was Jake's choice. Tess pushed against his side. 'And another small tin of red,' he remembered. Surely now nobody could have any reason to complain. But as they left the shop he noticed Jake was sulking. 'Small tin, large tin,' he muttered. 'What about 3.87 fifth's of a pint?'

Christ, William thought, is there no end to it? And then right in the middle of the road Tess yelped and clutched at her side. William spun round and dropped one of his tins. The top popped open and red paint slooped out on to the road. 'The letter!' Tess yelped. 'I forgot about the letter!' She dug her hand into her shorts and pulled out a cream envelope.

'Tess!' William shouted and he saw the familiar blue hand. He stooped down for the paint and a car honked loudly, shooting pain into his ear. 'Get across!' he yelled to the children. 'Get out of the road!' But Jake had already seized the letter and was tearing at the envelope to get inside. 'Put it away,' William shouted. He could see people staring and he realized red drops of gloss were spattering his shoes. 'Put it away and get into the van.'

'Dear Jake and Tess . . .'

The letter in their father's envelope wasn't from Victor, but from Min. They turned away from William on the long front seat as Tess whispered the words. 'Would you like to come on holiday? Me and V are going on the boat. It would have to be this weekend because we're going to Ireland. Please say yes.' There was a sketch of two small children with very messy hair. They had balloons beside their mouths and in each balloon was 'YES'.

Tess and Jake both laughed. The way Min had written it the word looked like Hurray.

William could feel them looking at him. Tess's face was wide open and Jake was pale with hope. 'Can we?'

William couldn't help it, his whole insides felt sick. The paint was hardening along his leg and his right shoe, his sailing shoe, was ruined. All he could think of was Felicity, her arms wrapped round her new baby, sitting in a huddle with his girls. 'No, you cannot,' he told them. 'This weekend we'll be finishing the caravan.'

'But – ' A rush of whining, sobbing noise leapt up. 'NO!' He pushed it down and he clutched hard against the wheel. 'When you set out to do a job, the job has to be done properly.' There was a rolling silence and to fill it William said, 'And I don't want to hear another word.'

Francine was lying down when they got back. The hospital had told her to be careful. Her blood pressure was high, and she was in danger of developing pre-eclampsia. William told the children not to bother her. 'Go out and play,' he told them, 'or write to that . . . Nin, and tell her, no, you can't just suddenly flit off to Iceland.'

Tess started to giggle. She couldn't help it. She bent over and put her hand over her mouth. But Jake was white with rage. He stormed into their bedroom and looked round for something to hurt. 'Oh God!' He tilted his head backwards and, letting his mouth fall open, he bellowed like a bear. The animals around the room looked stunned. They seemed to stare at Jake as if he'd used up all their noise.

'Jake,' Tess didn't know what to say. She wanted to comfort him, be exactly on his side, but she knew that something in her also wanted to see the caravan finished.

'I'd like to stamp on a glass cello,' Jake moaned. He lay

down on the floor and banged his head against the wood.

Tess sat on the bed, coughing to cover up the plastic rustle of the sheet. 'Yes, but afterwards, just think, you'd have to sweep it up.'

Jake lay very still as if her words had stifled him. 'Let's run away.'

'To Scotland?' Tess asked. She'd been thinking about Felicity and the bright cloak of her hair. About the room with the stone window and Sandy's master collection of bogeys, the greatest in the world. There was a karate room, Doon said, and a meditation room in the attic where you weren't supposed to think of anything at all. Jake didn't hear. 'We'll save any money, any money we might find . . . it won't be stealing really, just saving. And then as soon as we have enough, we'll walk to East Grinstead and get the train.'

'Yes,' Tess said, her heart beating fast and painful. 'But hadn't we better finish the caravan first?'

It took them two weeks to save the money. First they opened Tess's piggy bank and counted the insides, then they chose a long flat knife and took it up to Honour's room. Her money box was on a shelf behind her books. It was made from clay in the shape of a house and the only opening was a small slit in the roof.

'How does the money come out?'

'You're meant to smash it when it's full.' Jake picked it

161

up and raised it to his ear and shook it. Inside there was the beguiling sound of paper rustling. Paper rustling against coins. Jake slipped in the knife and tilted up the box. Two pence slipped out and dropped on to the floor. 'Pathetic.' He jammed the knife in again and tried to squint into the dark. Then he tipped the box upside-down and shook it, until fifty pence slid out.

They took a pound from each girl's box. Sandy's came mostly in grimy two-pence pieces. From Doon's they almost got a note. It peeked out and when they tried to snatch it with their fingers it slipped back in again. By the time they'd finished, the knife was hot and bent and they had to take it into the workshop and flatten it back into shape.

No one had ever known such a hot summer. Tess could smell the heat when she woke, baked and shimmering, collecting in each corner of the house. 'What bad luck.' Francine stood by the tap, splashing the water over her face, her neck, her swollen bosom, and her arms. 'Of all the summers . . .' and she fanned herself with a rush table-mat, leaning against the sink.

But at least the caravan was finished. Even Jake stood back to admire it. The outside was green, a gloss clover-green, and the window frames were red. The steps leading up to it were striped in orange and Jake had painted a leopard leaping above the door.

'It is beautiful.' Francine came out to see and she put her arms round Tess and Jake. 'What a lot you've learnt,' she smiled, and she gave William a tender look of thanks.

William was making lasagne as a special treat. He cleaned the kitchen, rolled up his sleeves and started on the sauce. He'd promised Tess she could help him arrange the layers. He boiled the strips of pasta and laid them out on every surface to drain. He diced the mozzarella, grated the cheddar and stirred spinach into the sauce instead of meat. 'Tess, where are you?' Usually she was hovering, her awkward, grubby body pressing in too close. 'Tess!' He stood at the back door and wiped his hands on the apron. 'Tess!' He could do the layers himself, had the perfect excuse to go ahead without her, a layer of sauce, a layer of cheese, a latticing of pasta, but instead he strode through into the wild. He was surprised to find the chickens hadn't been let out. It was nearly lunchtime and they were squawking and scratching at the door. He slid the bolt for them and watched them tumble into the day. The bantams were sleek and gleaming, Chanticleer rippling blue-black, the chicks filling out, the full fluff of their speckled feathers making them look fat. There was no doubt Tess had been doing a good job. The chicken hutch was clean with fresh new straw.

'Tess! Jake!' His voice came back at him through the trees. There was silence except for the squealing of Spotless behind his double-height wire fence. 'Odin?' he called, unsure exactly why, and the chickens crowded round him, forcing him to go back inside and bring them out a cup of corn. He threw it in an arc over the dry earth and, clucking and peeping, they pecked it up with savage joy.

The children weren't in the house, the workshop or the caravan, and usually they took Spotless if they were going up to the forest for a walk. Francine was sitting in the garden, a teaching-training manual propped up on her knees, although it was clear to William she would not be going back. For a moment she looked peaceful. She wasn't gasping or sweating or complaining of her back. 'One last ingredient,' he told her, and he strode towards the van.

'Come on, come on!' The wretched vehicle wouldn't start, and he had to roll it down the slope himself, hanging on to the steering wheel. He swung himself up just as it caught and he wondered what people did without their children. Eventually he rattled out over the cattle grid, pushing in the choke, pressing down on the accelerator and forcing the van up to its full speed. Mrs Newland was just turning in as he pulled out, the boot where her dogs usually sat piled high with Sainsbury bags. He flashed his lights at her, ignoring her hostile face, and it was only then he noticed he still had an apron draped around his neck.

William drove fast, scanning the countryside, slowing imperceptibly at the mouths of lanes, and peering over low hedges into fields. By the time he arrived at Twelve Ashes he was beginning to feel like a fool. Tess and Jake were probably at home. They were probably writing letters to Cyril Littlewood, plotting how to raise money to protect the tusks of elephants, or weaving beads into bracelets to sell. Anyway, it would have taken them all morning to walk here by road. But he carried on, driving out through the village, taking the van more slowly as he looked for a place to turn. And then there they were, trailing along in single file, Tess with her head down, plodding diligently, Jake striding on ahead, his mouth open, his chin up, singing. William drove a little past them and pulled on to the verge. He watched Jake's face in the side-view mirror as he realized, slowly, that he couldn't get past.

William leant over and swung open the door. 'Want a lift?' And at that moment Tess looked up, relieved. Without a word they clambered in. Jake stayed by the door so that Tess had to climb over him and sit between them. William turned the van round and in silence the three of them drove back to The Wild.

The day the Strachan girls came back it rained. The morning started with a haze of blistering blue, and Tess stood barefoot on the burning lawn and bounced a shuttle-cock up into the air. 'Play with me, Jake,' she called, but Jake had heard there was going to be a meeting of the local horse and hounds, and they were preparing to start their fox hunt from the triangle of green outside the pub. Jake stood in the kitchen melting aniseed balls in a saucepan. Aniseed smelt just the same as fox, and he planned to trail it round the countryside and save the fox's life. Tess watched him stir and stir his soup and imagined the huntsmen, so stout in their red jackets, thundering their horses the wrong way. 'Careful,' she said, worried that Jake might spill some on the Rayburn and that the whole hunt would race right through their house.

But then the sky began to darken and deep clouds meshed across the sun. Tess ran out to see it happen and William held his fingers to the sky. 'Yes,' he yelled, when a speck of rain, the first, brushed past him, and he held his face up to catch the feathery raindrops on his tongue. There was a far-off roll of thunder and a streak of lightning cracked open the sky.

'Dad! Daaaad! Daddy!' Honour, Sandy and Doon were scrambling up the ramp, the rain flying at them sideways, making their movements awkward as old film. 'We're back!' They threw themselves at William. They had new dresses on and their faces and their arms were freckled gold. Felicity stood behind them with the baby in her arms. 'Hello,' she said and tiny drops of rain shimmered in her hair.

'Isn't it wonderful?' Francine exclaimed, spreading her arms out and letting the water darken the colour of her dress. 'Just what we need.'

William looked over at Felicity and started taking off

his clothes. He pulled his T-shirt up over his head with one swift movement, and kicked his shorts into the flowers. His pants were black and clinging and he had to roll the sides to pull them down. Francine laughed and looked away, but Felicity just stared. 'Oh God,' she said.

'Can I do a rain dance too?' Sandy began, pulling off her dress. 'Forward march!' William yelled as another clap of thunder made them jump. He raised his knees into the air and marched. Soon Doon was naked too, her thin hard body narrow as a branch, and she skipped and danced behind her sister, flipping up her feet to catch the rain.

Tess didn't want to be left out. She was bigger than the other girls, plumper, and dark brown in stripes where the sun had marked the edges of her clothes. Quickly she pulled off her vest, and kicked her shorts into the air. The rain was full of breezes. They sidled in over her chest and up around her legs. 'Jake!' she called, throwing out her arms. 'Jake!' But he was still in the kitchen, stirring his aniseed soup. The warm rain pricked the dry skin on Tess's elbows and knees. She stuck out her tongue, thirsty suddenly, wanting the water to pour in torrents into her mouth, her eyes, her ears.

'Come on, Honour, come on!' William was calling, and carefully Honour began to fold away her clothes. They watched her as they marched, singing and twisting and following their leader whichever way he went. Honour's long legs were knock-kneed with shyness and she bent her arms over the tiny swollen bumps of her breasts. 'OK,' she said and she ran through the rain to join them. They marched twice round the lawn, whooping and yodelling, and then William led his procession through the vegetable garden to watch the plants open up their leaves. 'Mind you don't get pecked,' William called then as he pushed open the door in the old wall that led through to the chickens. There were splinters here, and twigs, and they slowed down to stoop, still squealing, under the low trees. They marched round to the front of the house, all jumping up to look through the windows at Jake sweating over the hot plate of the stove. 'Come out!' William called, but Jake pretended not to hear. Tess ducked down as they passed their neighbours' fence, in case Major and Mrs Darlby were standing on their path, watching the storm, counting out the seconds for each lightning mile.

When they got back to the lawn, Francine and Felicity were standing on the workshop steps, sheltering Abraham from the rain. They were talking hard and fast as if they'd known each other for years.

'Join us, ladies, join us,' William said, starting in on a new song, but the two women carried on. 'In Dublin's fair city, where the girls are so pretty,' he roared with his procession through the thick blanket of rain, falling heavier now and colder, and Tess tried to avoid looking at the swinging mass of pink, the grizzled hair, that hung between his legs.

'Daddy.' Doon and Sandy were shivering, their small

pale bodies battling through the rain. William slowed as he marched them into the bathroom where he ran the water low so that everyone could pile into the bath. Small burs and blades of grass floated in the water, and Honour, Doon and Sandy squashed against William's knees, chatting and squirming as they told him all their news. There wasn't room for Tess, but she had grass stuck to her legs and her shoulders were cold too. She sat up on the panel by the wall and squashed her legs behind Doon's back. No one seemed to notice her and eventually she climbed back out.

'So,' William was dressed again, and Francine and Felicity had come inside, 'will you be staying with us long?'

Felicity put a hand over her mouth as if she'd forgotten. 'Pete's waiting for me at the cattle grid . . . I told him I wouldn't be more than five minutes.' She looked warningly at William, who was beginning to whine. 'Oh come on,' she said, 'you know that I can't drive.'

'But we're having savoury pancakes.' He looked over to where they had been prepared, laid out in two neat rolls, lying in an earthenware tray, ready for the oven. 'No!' Spotless had been at them. The insides were torn wide open, sweetcorn, tomato, peppers, all chewed and splattered, dribbling out on to the floor. 'Jake, you've been in here all afternoon – Jake!'

His girls had followed him, dripping in their towels, and when they saw his darkened face they stopped, alarmed.

'That blasted dog!' He turned to Honour, but seeing her face, her shoulders flinching, he pulled her to him and held her close against his side. 'I wanted it to be special,' he bent low to explain, and he realized that she was the only person really who would understand.

'Mummy! Mummy!' Doon and Sandy were jumping at Felicity, trying to stop her from backing out, and when William turned he saw how small they really were. Their hair had lightened over the summer and they looked like buttercups, all eggcup yellow in their towels.

'Babies.' He stooped down and tried to catch them in his arms. 'Look at you.' But Doon had hold of Felicity and wouldn't let her go.

'I suppose the hunt will be called off now.' Jake slammed his saucepan down on to the side, and splashing the ruin of the pancakes with thick drops of aniseed, he siphoned the mixture into an empty jar.

This year Tess's classroom was going to be blue. It was a bright, dense watercolour blue that she'd admired more than anything when Jake was in Class Five. Jake was moving from purple towards pink, a calming colour that would lead him eventually into the neutral classrooms of the Upper School. Sandy was nearly six but she was still in Kindergarten. 'All my friends in Cammothmore can already read and write.' She kicked against her bench and William explained to her that if you were patient, and bided your time, then knowledge and skill would drop into your hands. 'But what about – ' She looked straight across the table, and Jake, catching her eye, glared back at her with such ferocity that she shuddered under her fringe.

In Kindergarten they drew with blocks of wax, rectangles in every colour but black. Tess wondered sometimes what they did with all the black. Maybe they built a great wax mountain, or kept them in a cupboard in the teachers' room, saving them up until you reached fourteen. At fourteen you went into the Upper School and then you were allowed to draw with anything you liked. With painting it was different. With painting you started in Class One with yellow. You were allowed one sheet of paper and this was soaked and plastered to a board, so that when you put the yellow on, it sank and swirled and turned the yellow into every kind of shade. The yellow shimmered, rippling in a watery gloss, and then it dried into a flat and grainy picture where the colour had built up. Sometimes one painting could last for several weeks. It was dried, and soaked, and painted over, so that after a whole year it was a shock when blue was introduced. Their first blue and yellow pictures were displayed around the walls and they looked like a double row of fried eggs swimming in the sea.

Jake disapproved of George House's attitude to art. At home he had a secret store of felt-tipped pens in garish colours, and he copied wild animals from his wildlife magazines. Tess admired the detail, the hard, clear lines, but even when she tried she slipped back into mottled skies, shimmering grasslands and small smudged figures with lopsided arms. If she needed anything specific, hair or grass or leaves, she had to call out for Mr Paul, who stooped down with his brush and swept her paintings into shape. He lapped up the colours, wetting the paper to bring the edges round, craning further and further forward until he'd slipped on to her chair. She leant against him, smelling the clean smell of his ironed shirt, the wave of his hair so neatly parted and his breath, so still and important as he worked.

At the end of the year she brought her paintings home, and there they were, identical, each one a tranquil light-filled landscape, swept into perfect shape by Mr Paul.

'William . . . I mean Mr Paul.' He was standing squarely against blue, and he looked up, serious, watching her run in. She wanted to tell him about the caravan, how they'd worked on it until it shone like new, but there was something in it, something desperate in the way Jake kicked the wheels, that made her stop.

'Was it nice in Cornwall?' she asked instead, and Mr Paul laughed. 'Yes, thank you very much.' He turned towards the board, and just under the tip of it Tess could see the white chalked edge of bones.

'Is it nearly time for Ragnarok?'

'You'll see,' he smiled.

'Soon?' She rolled up on to her toes.

'Not too soon.' And he pointed her into the room to find her desk.

Mr Paul told them about Cornwall, the cliffs and bays, the clotted cream, the pasties and the waves. 'What about King Arthur?' Tess asked. She wanted to know about the ruins of the castle where Guinevere had lived.

'Yes,' Mr Paul smiled. 'We visited Tintagel.' But Tess could tell he was waiting until next year to tell them what his own daughter already knew. 'Now,' he said instead, 'how did you get on with your homework?' And twenty children flipped open their books to show their pictures of Thor, the hammer, and the frost giant who wanted to have Freya for his bride.

Mr Paul rolled up his sleeves. 'Thor,' he whispered to pull their eyes to his, 'wanted to travel east to Utgard to flex his strength against the giants. "However few they are," Thor said, "they are too many."'

Tess looked out of the window at the row of apple trees, where the fruit, red and wizened, clung to each branch. She could almost feel the wood, how it came away all plastery in your hand, the dryness of the bark under your nails. Loki went with Thor. Mr Paul was right, he could never resist adventure, and when they stopped to eat at a farmer's house, Thor slaughtered his own goats for meat and put them on the fire.

'Whatever you do, don't break the bones,' he told the farmer's family, but the farmer's son was so hungry that

173

he snapped one bone for the marrow when Thor had looked away. The next morning, Thor raised his hammer over the goats' remains and brought them back to life, but he found one of the goats was limping. 'Who broke a bone?' he asked, and he raised his hammer over the farmer, his wife, his son and daughter, intending to kill them all.

Tess pulled her eyes from the window. Mr Paul was pale. 'Have mercy,' he begged. Mr Paul had turned into the farmer. 'Have mercy on us all.' And amazingly Thor's anger simmered down. Instead of killing the whole family he took the son and daughter to be his servants, so that when he and Loki rode away on their goats, the farmer's children rode with them into the unknown.

At William's insistence, Francine made nettle soup. She took her gardening gloves, a basket and some scissors and wandered off to where the nettles grew, thick and dusty in the square of garden intended for Jake. Tess went with her. She held the basket while Francine pulled on her gloves. Weeds and nettles crept up from the hedge and half submerged the gardens. There were dandelions there, and buttercups and huge dark clumps of borage that tricked you into thinking they were pretty with their tiny starry flowers, but soon the flowers wilted and the roots clawed deep, leaving the leaves to drag the garden down. Out of the five flowerbeds it was only Tess who'd really worked at hers. She'd grown radishes and carrots, nasturtiums that sprouted gratifyingly almost overnight, and marigolds to keep greenfly away from the blue rose. But the blue rose when it flowered was disappointingly mauve. Tess sent a petal to her father and he wrote back saying that until now he'd never believed in mauve. 'I send my heartfelt sympathies,' he wrote, 'and so does Min.'

Francine reached out for a nettle. The roots were long and knotted and didn't want to come and Francine had to squat down on the ground, her feet on either side of her belly to tug. She stopped occasionally when the sharp leaves flicked across her wrists and stung, and then Tess ran round collecting dock leaves to press against the raised bubbles of her mother's rash, wrapping the green pad like a bracelet to take away the sting. Francine flicked her wrist and blew and then, as if to take her mind off itching, she squatted back down on the ground and pulled some more. Tess snipped off the sweet tops of the nettles and dropped them into the basket and when they had a mound as high as the handle they carried them carefully back to the house. Francine mixed them with oil and potatoes, battening out the sting with milk, and when Tess peered into the pot she saw the dragon edges of the nettles mashed into a harmless soup.

Bless the tiny piece of ham,
Bless the lonely dab of jam,

Bless the sparsely buttered toast,
Father, Son and Holy Ghost.

Melody was back and she'd brought with her a new Grace.
'It's Scottish,' she told William when the others laughed.

'Welcome back, Melody,' he said, and Francine ladled
out the soup.

'Thank you so much.' Melody had changed over the
summer and every time William looked at her his mind
whirled with thoughts of limbs and breath and beaches.
Canvas and swimming trunks and sex.

'How was your summer?' he asked to stop himself
flushing.

'Just great.' Melody pushed the very tip of her spoon
into her mouth.

'We thought you'd go back into the cult.' Doon knelt
up on the bench.

'Well, I had other things to do.' She smiled and her
smile was luscious.

'So . . .' William was frightened she might go on into
descriptions, thinking theirs was the kind of household
which would welcome the details of such things. Melody
licked her spoon. Her tongue was extraordinarily pink.
'What is this, anyway?'

'It's, it's . . .' William sprinkled salt to try and rouse the
taste.

'It's nettle soup,' Jake answered for him. 'Without the
sting.'

And everyone except William laughed.

'It was William's idea.' Francine raised her shoulders at him. 'To welcome you back to macrobiotic life.'

'Mmmm, tasty,' Melody smiled. 'Actually, I've given macrobiotic up. It's too much trouble.' She twinkled her eyes apologetically at William. 'Now I've discovered other things in life,' she said. And she pushed her bowl to one side.

Jake wanted to train the girls as hunt saboteurs. He took his bottle of aniseed, half congealed, and trailed small drops behind him as he walked. He showed the girls the tracks and dented footprints where the horses ran, and then he veered off on to the golf-course. 'A fox wouldn't head off over open land,' Honour told him, but Jake dripped thick yellow drops across each green and poured a sticky measure down beside the flags.

Today the golf-course was deserted and the bracken was rusting back to red. Mushrooms had sprung up along the lanes, mysteriously thick and spongy as if they'd grown out of the damp. There were lopsided brown and yellow toadstools with undersides like fins, and others that were dense and slimy where they pressed against the ground. Right by the mouth of the lane was a red and white cluster, spotted and terrifying, luring you towards them like Hansel and Gretel's witch. 'You can eat those, you know,' Jake told them, but even he walked on.

When they reached the smooth dense plateau of their favourite green, Doon stretched out her arms and did a handstand and Sandy copied her, their straight thin bodies shooting upright, their hair, all mouse and tatters, falling upside down into the ground. Tess tried a cartwheel, her legs flailing, the whole sky tipping round. She spun and spun until she noticed Honour, her long legs crossed, sitting perfectly still while she wove grasses in a braid into her hair.

Sandy giggled and gasped, 'She's, she's, she's a smelly belly Tampax.' Tess saw there was a thin stain of blood spreading in a little heart against the seam of her shorts. Honour blushed and folded away her legs.

'Come on Tess,' Jake was pulling at her, but Tess wanted to sit close to Honour and learn to plait grass into her own hair. 'Oh, go on then,' he snarled and in desperation he turned to Sandy and, using her legs as a wheelbarrow, he drove her roughly over the green.

'How long does it last?' Tess could hear Honour, whispering to Melody in her room.

'Your period? Let me think, until you're about – fifty-four.'

'Really!' Honour gasped. 'I didn't know.'

'You have to use these, there's a sanitary towel and a Tampax.'

Tess could hear Honour pushing down the handle of

their door. 'Not at the same time of course.' Melody laughed.

'Oh, I see.' Honour walked back out through their room. Her shoulders were hunched, and she kept her head down as if she couldn't see.

'Goodnight,' Tess called to her, and Jake squirmed uncomfortably in his bunk.

Spotless had learnt to jump over the top fence. It was incredible to see him go, leaping like a great black log, gleaming as he vaulted, twirled and flipped his back over the wire. He landed hard, his four paws splayed and clumsy, but within a second he was up again, scooting off over the lawn, through the children's gardens and out on to the estate road. Sometimes they received angry letters from the Newlands. 'YOUR DOG HAS BEEN RUNNING WILD ON OUR LAWN,' Mrs Newland wrote in tiny capitals. 'CAN YOU KEEP YOUR PET UNDER CONTROL?' But more often Spotless would streak away across the fields, nosing under hedges until he found a flock of sheep. Spotless stretched his front legs out, lowered his head, his mock ginger eyebrows frowning in delight, and gave out a happy bark, and then he was off, racing round and round the animals, sending them into a frenzy of despair. Once Tess saw them running like a streak of porridge, pounding to the far corner of the field, and then Spotless raced ahead, barking at them as they tried to turn around. 'He doesn't hurt them,' Honour pointed out, but soon farmers, and then even a policeman, were knocking on their door.

'They hate us,' William said, scooping up a huge mouthful of rice. 'It's because we're letting the side down with our van. You can bet if we had a Volvo, they'd be inviting us for sherry on the lawn.' But he did warn Honour that Spotless might be in real trouble. 'It's the law,' he told her gently. 'The law of the land that dogs that chase sheep must be put down.'

To keep him under control the children walked Spotless every day after school. They took a bag and as they went they picked grass for the guinea-pigs to eat. Sometimes Jake stopped and chalked words across the phone box. One word in each pain of glass. 'I LOVE WHALES.' It was the only time he wrote. And then in the other boxes he put PISS and HATE.

William stormed into the house. He was late home after a parents' evening. 'Jake,' he said. He took a bucket and a cloth and twisted on the tap. 'Get down there and wash it off.' Tess could see his whole body wanting to jerk out of control.

'I thought you were a revolutionary,' Jake said and Tess's heart flipped over with fear.

William moved towards him.

'Tess!' Francine stretched her arm across the table

where they were all waiting to say Grace. 'Tess, go down as well and help Jake wash it off.'

'Be sure and do a good job now.' William watched them go and he kicked at the spots of soapy water trailed across the floor.

'What I don't understand,' Jake said as they walked down the steep hill, 'is how he knew it was me.'

The next day Tess had a stomach-ache. It started in mainlesson when they were illustrating the story of the giant king's cat. When Thor tried to lift it as a challenge it arched its back so steeply it made a rainbow curve over his head. The pain was low and aching and she asked Mr Paul if she could go and see Miss Glot.

'Come in, Tess.' Miss Glot had other patients, a boy clutching his mouth with toothache, and a girl in her eurythmy shoes waiting patiently for a copper rod. 'Oh Tess,' Miss Glot called over her shoulder as she rummaged for a clove, and Tess stepped forward, eager, wondering what she'd have to say. 'Tess, I've been meaning to ask you, are you still wetting your bed?'

Tess froze. 'No,' she gasped out on a laugh. 'No I'm not.' She could see the surprised eyes of the two children watching her, unsure. Tess backed out of the room. She didn't have a stomach-ache. She didn't need Miss Glot. She ran back across the playground with her blood still as a lake.

'All right now?' Mr Paul smiled at her as she slunk into the room, but she couldn't look at him in case he knew.

That night Tess sat on the cold black-plastic toilet seat three times before she went to bed. She sat and stared around her at the whitewashed walls, begging the last drops of water to come trickling out. But when she woke up in the morning her bed was just as wet. There were stains, and wider stains, like the rings around a tree.

'Don't cry.' Jake jumped down from the top bunk and Odin mewed in consternation and brushed his furry face against her cheek. Don't cry, don't cry, he seemed to say and he pushed his nose into her neck and used his whiskers to tickle round her chin. Tess wrapped her arms around him and squeezed so hard she felt him exhale in a little puff, but he bore it, letting his legs go limp while she pressed his warm body against hers.

'Your porridge will be cold, and even more delicious,' Jake warned, easing his cat out of her arms, and Tess let go reluctantly of Odin, and pulled the wet fringes of her nightdress up over her head.

'Does it have to be on the first Friday of half-term?' Francine lowered herself on to William's mattress where the Indian bedspread goddess entangled her with pale-blue arms.

William sighed. 'It does, I'm afraid.' He was taking his drama group to London. There were only ten of them, the numbers having dwindled since the heady days of last term when during an open-air production Alison, his one hope for a star, had forgotten her own newly improvised lines. But now Melody had joined them and he was taking them to see *The Passion Play*, a new version of the story of Christ in which a small bald Yorkshireman played God.

Francine moved her weight wordlessly to one side and William reached across her for his book. 'It'll be all right,' he told her, but she didn't speak.

As soon as William was on the train he began to worry. Could the baby come six weeks early? Of course it could, and Francine with no telephone and no one to drive. A wave of tenderness came over him and he promised him- he'd take all five children out the next day for a sail.

'Mr Strachan?' It was Simon with his feet up on the seat. 'William,' he corrected, and the girls, including Melody, began to giggle.

'What is it?' William said, hoping to join in, and Melody pointed out his zipper was undone.

Melody was changing every day. She'd found a way to straighten her red hair, and instead of frizzy it hung silk flat over her ears. When she laughed it swished from side to side, and then with both her hands she'd twist it up to show the sleekness of her neck. Since Melody had given up health food she seemed to eat nothing but peanut-butter-and-honey sandwiches, which she took to school three deep. It seemed to suit her. She'd lost her wholesome weightiness and instead had turned into a languid, syrupy vision of a girl. 'If Big Daddy could see her now,' William once remarked, and Francine laughed with him, although her eyes looked sharp.

'Mr Strachan? Mr Strachan? Where shall we go now, Mr Strachan?'

They were in Leicester Square, being pushed and squeezed, and William drew in a deep breath of grit and fumes. Beside him a man selling papers yelled out a long incomprehensible drawn-out name.

William looked round. It was so long since he'd been here. 'Right, this way, let's try up here.' He led his students up a side-street, trailing along a row of Chinese restaurants with the carcasses of ducks flattened against glass. There were shops with vegetables pouring out on to the street and supermarkets full of pale-pink packages and shiny implements of tin.

'William, where now?' one of the girls asked him and she sidled up alarmingly close.

'Ummm . . .' He put his arm on hers as if to steer her, but really he was stalling for time. 'This way,' he began and he led them through a dank back alley past a drunk, sleeping upright against a wall. 'No, sorry.' He had to take them back and he noticed the girls had all linked arms. It'll do them good to see a bit of life, stuck away in their privileged home county, but he felt himself shaking slightly when they crossed Shaftsbury Avenue just before a fire engine came hurtling by.

As they walked they glanced into the theatres. They had red plush foyers and huge signs lit up by lights. 'I saw a play here when I was about your age,' he swaggered, and he remembered the terror of coming down from Aberdeen with Felicity, meeting her parents on the steps. He still had the programme somewhere, and it made him think of Felicity and how she'd spread it over her lap to hide the bulge. Afterwards they'd eaten fish in a restaurant and the strength of it, the rich dense whiteness of the meat, had made him reel. 'Oh yes,' he pushed out his chest, 'I used to haunt this part of town,' and he led them into Soho, fingering the address of a small pizzeria he had copied out of the *Guardian*.

'Mr Strachan, Mr Strachan.' It was Simon and he was pulling back. 'I think we've lost Hilary.'

'What!' And just at that minute, just as he was spinning round in terror, he caught sight of Victor. 'Simon, look for her,' he ordered, lowering his voice, and without knowing why he tried to hide himself against the wall. Victor was sitting at a table, his legs stretched out, his arm around the shoulders of a girl. They were out on the pavement although it was November and they were drinking coffee in small cups.

'Here she is, here she is,' his students chanted, and squealing and skipping they crowded round like tourists. William herded them over the road and into the pizzeria, where from the front window he could look right across at Victor, his shoulders silently shaking, laughing and laughing with his girl. She was young, as young probably as William's students, with short pale tusselled hair, and when she stood up he saw she was as powerful as an elk. Her skin was parchment, her limbs proud and removed and he could imagine her belly, pale blue with a light peach dust of pink.

The *Guardian* was right. The pizzas were delicious. Made with thin Italian dough. He sat sideways at the end of the table and kept an eye on Victor as he ate. Why isn't he working at his writing? he thought, and he wished there was an authority he could report him to. Maybe he's doing research, he sneered and he tried to guess the age of the girl.

'Mr Strachan – I mean William – is the play about to start?'

William stood up in a hurry just at the moment Victor pushed back his chair. He had hold of the girl's elbow, and she was pulling away, scowling, trying to kick out. Can't you see? William thought, she doesn't want to go. But the girl turned and with no warning kissed him fully on the mouth.

'Right.' William paid the bill, folding and storing the receipt, and he herded out his charges, all ten of them, squealing and giggling, their arms unhelpfully linked, to walk down to Charing Cross and over the bridge to the National Theatre. He walked among them, keeping them all in his view, and as they walked he pointed out the sights. Trafalgar Square, just glimpsed beyond the traffic, the Houses of Parliament along the river from Big Ben. It was beautiful, so beautiful, the shimmering, oil-slick water, the bridges stretching with fairy lights to north and south. And then, dazzling, like a block of granite, there was the National Theatre, which he'd already decided he was going to like. But he was struggling. It looked so like a car park, and in just over a year his eyes had softened with the endless curves and arches of George House. 'Each slab of concrete has been pressed with planks of wood,' he directed the eyes of his students, who'd never seen such an expanse of grey, and as they looked they saw the pale indented marks of wood, the lines and knots and whirls of timber pressed against cement.

'We'd better find our seats.' He hurried them into the theatre, but this production was too modern and innovative for seats. The audience stood in the empty theatre, following the actors from scene to scene, making up the crowd of a medieval market-place, encouraged to jeer at Jesus Christ as he toiled by shouldering the cross.

'Isn't it fantastic?' He turned to Melody, realizing too late that his students had taken advantage of the inform-ality of this production to drift into the toilets to smoke.

'No chairs,' William shook his head as they travelled

back to Sussex on the train, and he thought how scandalized the Teachers' Association of George House would be.

It was William's turn for Christmas.

'But you had them last year!' Felicity's voice was breathy with disbelief.

'No.' William had been looking forward to this. '*You* had them last year.' There was a silence in which he could hear Felicity trying not to cry. 'You had them last year and I gave you the use of my home. Think about that.'

'Think about the children.' Felicity's voice was lined with ice. 'How will they feel?'

There was a pause and then the pause was filled with the hurry of the pips. William pressed in more money. 'It was you who deserted them,' he rushed in as the money cleared into more space. 'How did they feel then?'

'I never deserted them, I deserted you!' Felicity screamed back. 'I went off for a weekend! For a weekend, that's all!'

Neither of them put down the phone.

'You can have them at Easter. For ten days,' William said then more kindly and Felicity began to sob. William put the receiver close to his ear and the sound of her crying soothed him.

'But will they be all right?' She was defeated. 'Without their mother for so long?'

'They'll be fine. They are fine. We're doing a fantastic job, Francine and I.'

'I'll send presents,' she said, her voice breaking, and William offered, 'If you want more time you can always go back to the courts.'

There was a long silence while they listened to each other's breathing, unable to believe that for years and years they had been friends. Then Felicity put down the phone.

Francine was resting in bed. 'But wouldn't it be nice,' she ventured, 'wouldn't it be nice to have some time . . . a little time – ' She broke off when he looked at her.

'How would you feel,' William stood over her. 'How would you feel waking up on Christmas morning alone?'

'But you wouldn't be alone,' she prompted him. 'You'd have . . . you'd have Tess and Jake.' She looked down at the taut skin of her stomach. 'You'd have me.'

'Yes.' William knelt down on the bed, and laid his hand on the fierce heat of her skin. There was a ripple as the baby kicked under his hand.

'Did you feel that?' Francine laughed, and the baby kicked again.

'It hates me already.' William tried to find its foot, to feel the little jolt that meant new life. 'It's gone,' he said, 'it's gone,' and he curled up, exhausted, by Francine's side.

Tess had never seen so many presents. They were piled three deep below the tree. Occasionally Tess inspected the labels. 'To Honour, love Mummy.' The kisses went round the label like a tail. 'To Doon, love Mummy.' 'To Sandy.' There was something small and squashy that felt like a doll. 'For Big Mummy, love BIG Dad.' When Jake saw it his lip curled up. 'That poor kid,' and he went back to their room to find his Spiderman comic in its hiding place under his clothes.

Comics were against the rules of George House. Any kind of comic, television or cartoons. They stunted the imagination and stopped you thinking for yourself. There were probably other things that were forbidden but Tess hadn't even heard of what they were. Once, for three months, they'd lived in a house that had a television. The owners kept it on a round table, covered by a cloth, and once a week the vase of flowers was taken off it and they were allowed to watch *Blue Peter* if they promised not to beg for anything else. But *Blue Peter* wasn't so very interesting, and she never understood why you'd want to make dolls out of toilet rolls when there was wood and wool and clay.

'I hate Christmas,' Jake said and he made Tess come out with him into the field across the road. He sat down on the sawn stump of a tree and pretended to retch.

'Jake, don't,' Tess said.

William had made them open their presents in the order of their birth. One by one, a package was brought into the fireplace and everyone craned forward to watch as the wrapping was peeled off. It was fun for the first round, and the second, with Sandy and William overlapping at the beginning and the end, but then the waiting, the longing, the itchiness of suspense began to make Tess sad. Felicity's presents had been overlooked as inferior, but soon it became impossible to hold them back. Honour adopted a nonchalant expression as she ripped at hers, and Sandy, to outdo her, frowned as she pulled away the string. William rewarded them both with an indulgent smile. But Doon couldn't pretend. 'Oh look!' Her eyes filled up with tears. 'How lovely,' and she pulled a gossamer-fine waistcoat, crocheted from silk, out of its bed of tissue. 'I'll wear it now,' she said and she pulled it on hungrily, covering the hand-stitched corduroy of her Christmas dress.

And then Jake's presents ran out. 'Oh Jakey,' Francine bit her lip, 'that's terrible,' and Tess saw her glance at William to stop. But William jumped up and reached under the tree, scrambling on his hands and knees, reaching with his long arms for the endless gifts, until his girls sat in a sea of tissue, fattened up and gasping with the glut.

Jake pulled Tess's hand and led her through a field, the grass wetting them to the knee and turning the leather of their shoes slick black. Eventually they climbed out through the hedge right by the bus-stop. It was a small shelter set back from the road and if you sat inside it you could only see the bus after it had passed. 'Come back! Come back!' you had to shout, but the bus had always turned the corner by the church. The bus shelter was in memory of a child. There was a small plaque, and however many times they read it it always made them laugh. IN MEMORY OF OUR BELOVED DAUGHTER, GAYNOR POGLIN. Even now Tess and Jake put their hands over their mouths. 1958–1969.

It was dark outside the shelter and there was something soothing about knowing no bus was going to come by. 'Let's go up on to the golf-course,' Jake said, and Tess gripped his arm as they stepped into the dusk. They walked along the lane beside the stream, heard the water rushing over tiny stones, and smelt the brackish iron smell of the underground spring. It was cloudy tonight and they couldn't see a single star, but the lights were on in the Jenkinshaws' house, and putting his finger to his lips Jake climbed over their fence. A dog began to bark but Jake ignored it.

'Jake, don't!' Tess felt sickened and afraid. 'What are you doing?' She watched as he snaked forward through the vegetable patch and pressed his face against the glass. The dog was silent, its yapping snuffled to a growl, and Jake stayed pressed against the window. Tess waited, willing him to come back, when she was startled by a shout. It was a dark high shout of shock, and Jake leapt back from the window and, running, flung himself over the battered fence. He pulled hard on Tess's arm and hurled them both under a bush.

A second later Mr Jenkinshaw rushed out. He had something in his hand, and when he swung around Tess saw it was a gun. It was a long wooden rifle, the silver of the barrel glinting in the light. Mr Jenkinshaw put the gun up to his shoulder and, turning slowly, he aimed it straight at them from the hole that was his nose.

Tess tried not to breathe. She could feel Jake's body, rigid with quiet, and when she glanced at him she saw he'd closed his eyes. Tess closed her own eyes too and they lay like that for what seemed like hours.

'He's got a wife,' Jake whispered to her when finally they heard the latch of Mr Jenkinshaw's front door. 'She was in her dressing-gown with her feet up on a stool. I promise she was just reaching over for a mince pie when she saw my face pressed against the glass.' Jake rolled on to his back and stretched his arms and legs. 'How long is it, do you think, since Mrs Jenkinshaw last saw a nose?'

'Shhh!' There was silence all around them, and the last light in the Jenkinshaw house went off. 'Can we go?' Tess asked. Her clothes were wet and she was shivering with cold.

'I suppose we'll have to.' They struggled up out of the bracken and, ducking down along the lanes, they hurried as quickly as they could towards home.

★

'Tess, that's not nearly enough.' It was her turn to help with supper and William had asked her to grate carrot for the salad. Raw carrot gave you energy and should be eaten if possible at every meal. Francine was laying the table while Doon and Sandy filled eggcups with pepper and salt. Honour was feeding Spotless, cutting black clots of meat straight from the butcher, slicing and pronging them on to his dish.

'Mum, are you all right?' Tess asked, as Francine turned away. She had her hand over her nose and her throat looked full. The baby was now exactly one week late.

'Tess,' William's voice was stern as he prodded each baked potato. 'Tess, I was talking to Miss Glot today and I don't understand why you told her you'd stopped wetting your bed when it's clear to everyone you haven't.'

Tess had just slipped a sultana into her mouth. She didn't know why, because she didn't even like sultanas and it was William who'd asked her to put them in the salad. William was watching her. Waiting for her reply. 'Tess?' The room was very still. The sultana swelled sickeningly in her mouth, and when she went on grating she grated the soft edge of her finger in a slice. The skin was white with shock, and as she watched, the blood rushed in and filled it up. Her chest was hurting, hardening, splintering in two and she almost gasped as it stabbed into her chest. But she carried on grating, the blood turning the carrot scarlet and then brown, the soft sloosh of the carrot falling down into the bowl. She could feel William looking at her, imagined the eyes of his three daughters flickering with disgust, and then her mother began to move towards her. Tess dropped the grater. She opened her mouth wide and screamed. She screamed and screamed. There was nothing else to do. And then, still screaming, she ran into the hall. She buffeted against the coats and boots, stumbling on the doormat, and hurtled on into the laundry room. It was dark outside, and inside there was nowhere to hide. She kept on screaming, not daring to stop in case someone tried to follow her, someone tried to see into her face, to see the girl stained yellow with old piss, who couldn't stop even though she was ten. More than ten. Ten and a half. Almost eleven. Her heart quaked, and drawing breath for a new scream she shut herself into the bathroom. It was the bathroom she was expected to clean and she saw a line of grime around the bath. There were soap scales lining the sink and the taps were clouded grey. For a moment she stopped screaming and in the sudden lull there was a knock on the door. She breathed in deep and in her terror she screamed right at the door. There was no lock on it, so she held the handle upright and leant into the wood. Her scream was rising, high above her ears, and below it she could still hear the rest of life murmuring on.

'Tess?' It was Jake. 'What happened?' She remembered with a sob of relief that Jake hadn't been in the room when William told. 'Let me in!' Jake rattled the door. But Tess couldn't stop screaming. 'OK,' she heard him sigh. 'Be like that.' And soon afterwards his footsteps died away.

The bathroom backed on to the kitchen, right against the wall where William sat on his one chair and she could hear the scrape as he sat down. She told him. She told him. Tess wanted to get hold of her mother and hurt her, and reeling with the pain she began to scream again in the quiet murmur that was Grace. But then underneath her screaming she heard Sandy laugh, 'Could someone change the record?' and Doon piped up, 'Maybe the record's stuck?'

Tess waited to see if her mother would laugh, but Francine wasn't laughing, she was leaning into the bath-room door. 'Come on, darling,' she soothed, 'it's not so bad.' Terrified she would force the door open, Tess rushed to the sink, filled the toothbrush jar with water and stood ready to throw it over her if she dared come in. 'Tess, Tess now.' But Tess scrunched up her eyes and screamed 'GO AWAY!' with such ferocity that even she felt shaken and afraid. There was a silence then, and after some minutes of shallow breathing, Francine went away. Tess stopped screaming and began to cry. 'I'll never feel sorry for her,' she sobbed. 'I'll never feel sorry for her again.' She leant over the basin and cried. She cried and cried, splashing water against her eyes and nose, and when she stopped there was silence from next door. She stood and listened. Nothing. And then someone tried to push the door. It opened just enough, and without seeing who it was Tess picked up the toothbrush jar and threw the water out.

'Arrgh!' It was Honour, and Tess jumped to think that she'd been got.

'Leave me alone,' she shouted gleefully, and she filled the jar with more water, hoping suddenly that someone else would try to push their way in. But no one tried again. The house was silent. There was no more laughter from the kitchen, no more benches scraping back. She had no voice left to scream so she wrapped herself in the bathmat and lay down on the floor.

She lay there for a very long time. She couldn't go to sleep in case she wet herself, so she just lay still and listened. She wondered what would happen when Jake needed to brush his teeth, and once she was roused by the flush from the upstairs toilet, rumbling through the pipes. But hours and hours passed and no one came into the bathroom. No one came to wash their face or hands, or give their hair a hundred strokes. It was cold under the bathmat, the floor was tiled and hard. Tess folded a towel and put it under her head. It occurred to her she could use this time to clean the bathroom, but then she remembered what everybody knew and her heart hardened and her mouth bunched up with tears. She lay very still until in the black night behind the window a bird began to sing. It was so loud and clear it sounded like a whistle, twittering, trilling, like a piper with a pipe. Tess struggled up. Her legs were stiff and her hip ached where it had pressed against the floor. She eased open the door, carefully, in case a silent sentry had been placed outside, and finding there was no one she tiptoed across to her own room and climbed into her bed. Odin was lying beside Jake, one eye open, waiting for her, as if for half the night he'd been wondering where she was.

She must have slept, because she was woken by Sandy charging through her room, her nightdress flapping, her hair tangled to a fuzz. 'You were meant to get us up!' she yelled to Melody, batting open her door. 'Mrs Beddoes is here to take us to school,' and skipping and twirling she rushed back out.

Jake swung his legs over the bunk. 'Sandy,' he called. 'Hey, you little twit.' But she'd already gone.

Melody put her head around the door. 'Get up, you two,' she yawned and her nightdress fell open to reveal one perfectly round breast.

Jake scowled and jumped down from his bunk.

'Where's Mum?' Tess asked. The sheet around her legs was dry, but her body ached and her eyes were thick and crusted up with glue.

Jake pulled a shirt over his head. 'They went to the hospital,' his muffled voice came back. He was unbuttoning it over his nose. 'She was just serving the baked apples when something happened.'

'The baby?'

'Of course the baby,' Jake said. His head popped through and he looked right at her. 'She started to crumple up.'

'I didn't mean – ' Tess tried to explain. Jake mustn't think she thought it was because of her. She hadn't hoped that. 'I didn't mean . . .'

Honour put her head round the door. 'Mrs Beddoes is waiting. If you want breakfast you'd better come now.' She looked at Tess still in her bed and nodded for her to hurry up. There was no sign or glimmer of the night before. No wet streaks from the water. No trace of revenge for the throwing of the toothbrush jar.

'All right.' Tess quaked with hope. Tears pressed up into her eyes. They'd all forgotten. They'd forgotten her, and her horrible secret, and if she kept quiet and hardly breathed it was just possible no one would mention it again.

Mrs Beddoes had an estate car with three rows of seats. 'Hup hup,' she said. 'You don't want to be late. Not today of all days.' She smiled so wide she crinkled up her eyes.

'Has – ?' Tess stopped herself before she asked, and anyway Mrs Beddoes was searching for Sandy's socks, checking Doon had her plimsolls for gym, and asking why, if Jake had music, he seemed intent on leaving his trumpet at home.

'Tess, are you all right?' Mrs Beddoes stopped without warning and peered into her face. 'You look all . . .'

Tess felt her blood go still and the other children seemed to hold their breath. 'I'm fine.' Tess fixed her gaze and quickly, brightly, she flashed out a smile.

'Right.' Mrs Beddoes huffed out a puff of air and all five of them climbed into the car.

Mrs Beddoes was a colleague of Miss Glot. She taught eurythmy to the lower school and had done so for twenty-five years. Eurythmy was a kind of dance where you always stepped toes-first. You stepped out rhythms and clapped your hands, and over years and years you learned to dance the alphabet with your feet. There were arm movements as well. A was a hard thrust, and B a wide circle where your fingers met and pointed back towards your chest. F flitted away from you like fire and for S you shuffled backwards in a curve. No one at George House really liked eurythmy, or if they did they kept it to themselves. Tess thought it was because of the eurythmy shoes. Eurythmy shoes were grey and snakeskin thin and they made your feet look hideous and flat. If someone had thought to make them pink or black, with trims of ribbon or a bow, no one would mind putting them on so much.

'Mmmm.' Mrs Beddoes exhaled now on a small flat note and she smiled through it as she drove. She slipped the gears smoothly into third.

'So did you hear from Dad?' Honour asked.

'Did you speak to Daddy at the hopspical?' Sandy asked.

Mrs Beddoes smiled. 'Yes, yes, there's no need to worry.' She tucked her chin down and pushed her bosom out.

'But, I mean – ' Honour's face was suddenly pale. 'I don't understand.'

Mrs Beddoes frowned at an overtaking car. 'These things take time,' she soothed. 'When your Daddy, your – ' she glanced round at Tess and Jake, 'your William rang, there was still no news.'

'Is Francine not having the baby anymore now?' Sandy asked and Mrs Beddoes patted her on the head. 'Patience, patience. All will be revealed.'

Jake threw a rolled-up piece of paper from the front. 'Fifty pence that it's a girl.'

'Jake!' Mrs Beddoes took a moment to resume her smile. 'As I said, there's no need to worry.' In silence they turned left at the church and glided up the last steep hill towards the school.

Mr Paul spoke slowly, gently, smiling at the drooped heads of his class. He dipped his voice low to draw the children in. But his story was too terrible, too terrible to hear, and Tess didn't want to know how Loki was shut up in a drawer. He'd disguised himself as a hawk, for no reason at all, and he'd been caught and thrown into a drawer. The giant who'd entrapped him had left him there for three whole months. He'd had no food or water and had lain in his own mess, and finally when the frost giant let him out he was too weak to speak.

'Are you all right, Tess?' Mr Paul had padded forward and was stooped over her desk. 'Are you all right, my dear?' He took out his own handkerchief and gave it to her to wipe away her tears. The bell rang and Tess wandered shakily out into the playground. She tried not to think about her mother crumpling up with a large spoon for serving baked apples still gripped in her hand. But when she forced herself away she only thought of Loki, so pale and thin and stinking, lying in his drawer. From now on I won't sleep, she told herself, I won't let myself be caught, and she knew it was her only choice.

Tess went out to lock up the chickens. Dusk was the hour when foxes crept out of the wild. A fox could rip and tear a chicken, and then throw it up into the air for fun. William had told them how in Scotland a fox had come and slaughtered a whole flock. 'He didn't even eat them.' William was disgusted. 'Just murdered them for sport.'

Tess pulled on her boots. 'Rebecca?' She felt anxious now. 'Henrietta?' The hens scuttled round her, clucking in out of the gathering dark. She crouched down and rustled her thumb against her finger, clucking to them to

lure the dawdlers in. She had to wait for Chanticleer
to saunter up, treading with high careful steps through
the undergrowth of leaves. 'Come on,' but Chanticleer
was a sleek oiled gentleman, his wings blue-black, his shirt
front rounded like a prow, and there was nothing you
could do to hurry him. Even his beak was shimmery and
his coxcomb, bright red and wavery, had the indentations
of a crown. The Marron chicks were large and round and
speckled, big blowsy chickens who dropped grey fluff
feathers and made baths for themselves out of dips of
dust. They were less sleek than the bantams, less gainly,
and Tess found she couldn't love them as much. She
stooped to lead them into the shed, holding her breath
against the hot dense smell, and showering out long handfuls of corn, while the chickens pecked and scratched and
scampered past her with their bony wings.

'Right, you can have whatever you want for supper,'
Melody told them when William and Francine still hadn't
returned, and Sandy and Doon danced around her clam-
ouring for pancakes with maple syrup. It was what she'd
eaten in America, she'd told them, the day that her mother
had kidnapped her out of the cult. They had driven
straight to a diner and ordered sausage, bacon, and pancakes dribbled with thick sweet maple syrup.

Sandy sat solemnly with her fingers pressed together in
an arch.

'Some hae meat, and canna eat,
And some wad eat that want it;
But we hae meat, and we can eat,
And sae the Lord be thankit.'

Everybody clapped instead of saying Amen and Sandy looked proud. 'I learnt it for Daddy,' she said, and then looked disappointed when she remembered William wasn't there.

Melody served the pancakes, sprinkling them with lemon juice and icing sugar, letting Jake drip golden syrup over his. As she ate, Tess held on to Odin, pressing him against her side. Odin mewed and struggled to get down. 'I mustn't sleep,' she whispered into his soft fur, the tiny beads of colour threading through each hair, and then Odin twisted away, his claws bursting in frustration from their pads and ripping into her arm. Tess gasped against the pain and Odin looked back at her reproachfully, as if to say it was her own fault for hugging him too long. 'Odin!' Tess tried to grasp his collar, but he closed his eyes slowly and gave a tiny smile before arching his body through the cat flap and slipping out into the night. I won't sleep, she promised, wrapping a dishcloth round her arm, and she remembered how the eggy smell of her classroom, the warmth of the soaked paper, had lulled her into a doze. 'Would you like to see Miss Glot again?' Mr Paul had roused her, and when she'd started awake with 'No,' he'd stooped down beside her and slipped

204

the paintbrush out of her hand. He'd wet it with water, softened the bristly hairs and turned the brush to a fine bright point of paint. Her painting was of the hawk, but her hawk had turned all mushy, its feathers more like fur, and as she watched, Mr Paul brightened her bird for her, making each feather curve down like the closed wood petals of a pine.

'Relax,' William said to Francine, who was holding on to the metal frame of the bed. 'Good girl, relax.' He knelt down beside her and put his hand sternly on her arm.

'Get off,' she slapped at him, and he stood up and strode towards the door, turned and came back, wishing he was allowed to wait on the other side of the wall. His own father would have laughed at him, laughed and told him he had no one but himself to blame. 'Wait in the pub with a cigar, you idiot.' And he wished now there was some way of finding that he could. A midwife came in and attached a monitor and there was a brief moment of calm between contractions as they heard the baby's heart, rushing and whirring in an underwater land. And then Francine's face whitened and her eyes screwed shut and William let her grip his hand. It was like the sea, washing in and in, and he wished it would crash right over them and take them both away. If only there was another bed, a place he could lie down, and when Francine, dizzy with gas and air, began to doze, he found himself envying the fact that, even for an instant, she could rest.

The hours leaked through into another night. He gripped Francine's hand and smiled at her. 'Come on,' he whispered. 'Come on.' His jaw was locked with waiting, but Francine just rolled and rolled with pain. Felicity had been a warrior. She'd taken up karate after Doon was born. Doon, so tiny and frail, had almost sucked the life from her, her small, wrinkled body unleashing a gush of blood so powerful that it bled every trace of colour from Felicity's face. William had watched as the nurses placed Doon in her arms and saw with terror how they seemed to cling together as if, through sheer love and lack of blood, they were about to drift away. He'd lose them both. Lose everything. Then as soon as Felicity recovered she took up karate, where on that first evening she met Pete. The first time William had seen them together they'd been locked in high-kicking combat, their white clothes belted red and yellow with their scores, and by the time Sandy was born Felicity was a leanly squatting creature, crouching down on a groundsheet without a midwife or a nurse. By now, he thought, she must be a black belt, and he imagined her crouching like a Cherokee Indian to give birth to Abraham behind a bush.

Francine began to howl. 'I'm here, I'm here,' William pressed her hand. Hot tears scorched her face and she started to tell him how alone she'd been with Tess. 'Victor was out somewhere, and I couldn't think where, and I waited and waited until the last minute but he never came. I had to get to hospital by taxi and when I arrived the midwife shouted at me for bringing Jake.' She was panting now, sweating, pounding on the wall. 'What was I to do with him? And then eventually when . . . when it was all over, when Victor finally arrived . . .' She beat her head into the pillow and pressed it there as a contraction started in her spine, 'I wanted to hate him so much.'

'But *I'm* here now, Francine, don't you see?' It didn't seem to make a difference. She was lost to him, riding on a bloody mangled wave. 'I'm going to have to – ' He motioned to the midwife and stepped out into the corridor and leant against a wall. The corridor was peaceful, beautiful even with its clear linoleum lines. Of course, he thought, of course, I can always walk away. At the far end was a telephone and he went to call Mrs Beddoes to ask if she'd mind collecting the children again that day. When he got back Francine was dwarfed by white-coated technicians. Her legs were up in stirrups, and there was blood dripping on to the floor. He closed the door as carefully as he could but Francine saw him and turned her head away. 'It's all right.' William took her hand, and their eyes fixed on each other as the doctor took a pair of gleaming silver forceps and slid them inside. William tried not to look. It seemed deceitful and improper, but he found himself strangely fascinated by the gore. 'We can't all be Japanese warrior women,' he found himself saying, and on Francine's rueful laugh the baby was pulled out.

'It's . . .' The doctor was swabbing and injecting while the midwife lifted the child. 'You've got a girl.'

'A girl.' William felt a knock like the boom pulling taut across a sail. 'A girl,' he tried to laugh. 'We've made a girl.'

The baby wasn't crying. She was watchful and still, wrapped in a white towel, ready to be taken away and weighed. William held his arms out for her and felt the tiny weight of the baby descend. She was wrinkled, mottled, her dark eyes swimming in her face, and William felt a great surge of panic burst up through him as if this being, this tiny little life, was just too much to bear.

But Francine was rousing, struggling to sit up. 'Where is she?' Her eyes were softening, her shoulders broad and sloping to steady out the new weight of her breasts. 'Where is she?' Her face was folding up in uncontrollable smiles. 'Give her to me.' She was holding out her arms.

'I'll just go off to phone,' William started up. 'I'll call the school.' He needed to speak to Honour. He needed to hear her clear, serious voice. To feel that he could call her away from her lessons, make her run right round the rhododendron island to where there was a telephone in the teachers' office of the school.

'No,' Francine gripped his arm, 'don't go.' She forced him to look into their baby's face. 'She looks like you. A native American . . . with Calvinistic roots.'

William sniffed. The baby was ugly as sin. 'Why do my

children always look like me, poor sods?' His lip curled down with sorrow.

'Stay with us a little while.' Francine held tight on to his arm. 'Stay with us?' And William felt himself about to cry.

Tess kept herself awake with little pinches and prods and when she caught herself slipping into sleep she crept out of bed and went into the bathroom. She looked at all the toothbrushes, William's flattened down and bristly, her mother's pale-purple silk, and the thick cluster of all the smaller ones, their heads crusty with toothpaste, rosemary and fennel, that hadn't been properly rinsed. Only Melody's was brightly striped and new. Maybe tonight she'd clean the window-ledge, polish the smears from the sink. But instead she wrapped a towel round her and sat down on the floor.

'Tess, what are you doing?' It was Jake standing over her, his face creased shut with sleep.

'Is it morning?'

'No,' he said and he stamped back off to bed.

Tess's knees creaked as she stood up and she wandered into the kitchen to check on the time. 'Go placidly amid the noise and haste, and remember what peace there may be in silence.' *The Desiderata* still hung above the Rayburn, its corners curling, its edges toasted brown. Tess let her eyes travel over its calming surface and rest on the last line. 'Be careful, strive to be happy.' She took a deep breath. It was only two-thirty in the morning. Tess pulled on her coat and opened the back door. A frost had settled on the garden, turning the mounds of earth lint white. The moon was full and ghostly and she wondered how her mother would be able to bear it when Tess refused to look at her when she came home. Then she saw Odin, his body balancing on the ledge of Lupin's cage, his tail whirring round for balance, and as he turned to look at her, she saw his broad face was clotted thick with blood. 'Odin!' She covered her own mouth, and he darted his head back into the cage and pulled out the body of a guinea-pig, its stomach torn right open, its throat ripped out. Odin looked at her, his eyes bright yellow in the light from the back door, and dropping Lupin, tattered and limp, he ran off into the wild.

Doon was wailing outside her window when she woke up, but all Tess could think of was that her sheet was dry. 'It was probably the fox,' she heard Honour say. 'He's only killed four of them, that's lucky really,' while underneath her comforting she heard Sandy counting and counting to see how many were still there.

Doon cried all the way to school. 'Did you forget to lock them in?' Mrs Beddoes enquired kindly and Doon put her head on to her knees and sobbed.

'It must have been a very vicious animal,' Jake gloated.

'A kind of vampire of the guinea-pig world.' Tess held her breath. 'Tearing out small squeaking hearts and sucking up the blood.'

'Don't,' Tess tried to quieten him. 'Shhh, Jake, please.' She opened her eyes wide to warn him but Mrs Beddoes pressed her shoulders down with a great sigh for emphasis and said, 'That's enough now, Jake.'

William had parked his van beside the wishing gate and the children saw him as they trailed through from school. Tess always wished the same wish, just in the centre as she pulled the hinged gate through, and quickly, with her eyes closed, she mumbled the wish now. William held up his hand and waved to them.

'Come on,' Honour was behind her, 'let me through.'

'Where's Mum?' Jake said, pushing at Honour, and Tess knew she should feel afraid. Where was she and why was William standing there so still?

'Daddy.' Doon and Sandy were running towards him, grabbing at his clothes, butting their heads against his thighs, but he was looking over their heads at Honour, holding his arms out to his oldest girl.

'You've got a little sister,' he told her, his voice apologetic, as if breaking some difficult news.

Tess felt herself swell up with joy. Smiles were rippling right through her, stretching at her mouth, her eyes, her nose. Her own sister. Her own. 'It's what I've always wanted.' She tried to find a way of flying against William, making him feel that she was pleased, but his own children were crowding in on him.

'We've called her Eve.'

There was silence for a moment. There had never been any talk of Eve, but at least it meant Tess didn't have to give Eliza back.

'The first woman,' Honour said.

'Yes,' Jake glanced at William, his eyes dark brown with cold, 'and hopefully the last.' He pulled open the back doors of the van. 'Honour,' he said, kicking in, 'you owe me fifty pence.'

When they got home Francine still wasn't there. 'They're keeping her in hospital for a few days.' William crossed her name off the rota. 'Jake,' he said, 'you're to help with supper.' But Jake was on the doorstep calling Odin. 'Odin!' He had a tin of cat food open in his hand, but Odin wouldn't come.

William still stood in front of the rota. He had his hands on his hips and he looked as if he were stuck. 'Jake,' he said eventually, drawing a deep breath. 'Jake,' and Jake turned to him, still holding the open can of food.

'I – it's – ' William was stumbling, trying to find some words for what he had to say. 'I think it's best that Odin goes away.'

'No,' Jake said.

'No,' William echoed him. 'You don't understand. I thought it best, for everyone, the other animals and the children, if an animal like Odin, really in fact vicious and wild, should go away.'

'I won't let him.' Jake was still clutching the tin of cat food, the jagged lid pressed against his chest.

William gave out a little irritated sigh. 'This afternoon I took him to a farm. He'll be happy there. It'll be for the best.' He turned away, and fixing his eyes on the larder walked quickly over to see what he could find for supper inside.

Jake stood very still in the doorway, the back door open, cold air streaming in. 'You can't,' he said. 'He's mine.'

William didn't answer. Only his legs were visible and the curve of his behind. 'Shut the door, won't you, Jake?' he called. 'There's a terrible draught.'

Jake stood completely still. Tess could see him thinking, understanding horribly there was nothing he could do, and she felt frightened for him, too frightened to take the cat food out of his hand. Eventually Jake moved over to the table, put the tin down and very quietly walked out of the room. William had had Odin put down. Tess knew this, just as Jake did. Any kind of idiot would know there was no farm.

William ducked out of the larder. He had two tins of chickpeas and a packet of rice. 'One day,' he said, smiling brightly, not realizing Jake had gone, 'we'll go and visit

Odin, see how happy he is in his new home.' But no one looked at him, and Doon, who was crouching with her back against the Rayburn, kept her eyes fixed on the floor.

Tess took as long as she could over the table. She straightened the knives and forks and laid spoons for pudding across the top. She filled the jug with water and polished the glasses with her sleeve. Eventually, when there was nothing left to do, she pushed open the door of their room. 'Jake?' At first she thought he wasn't there. But then she saw him lying on his bunkbed, the blanket pulled up to his chin. There was a dent where Odin was missing and Tess could see Jake's eyes were wide open, staring at nothing at all.

'I'll kill him,' he said, his mouth breaking, and he turned over on to his stomach and sobbed.

Tess tried to comfort him. She stood up on the ladder and stroked his hair. 'Get off!' he roared, 'get off,' and he flailed out with his arms.

Jake didn't come out for supper and no one asked why. The children ate in silence and Doon choked on a mouthful of rice. 'You should chew rice one hundred times,' William reminded her and Melody put down her fork. 'What is wrong with you guys?' She didn't know about Odin and the farm. She leant over towards William and smiled. 'They say only the most virile men father so many girl children.' Melody nudged his elbow, and William asked if she'd like to join him in a celebratory glass of wine. 'I'm exhausted,' he told her, his shoulders drooping with the first long sip, and he let his head fall forward dramatically on his chest.

'Big Daddy,' Melody crooned. 'This'll help cheer you up.' She tipped the bottle towards him and re-filled his glass to the brim.

Tess could tell Jake wasn't asleep. 'Goodnight,' she whispered, but he was much too still. Eventually he swung his legs over the bed. 'Come with me,' he said.

Tess was pleased to have an excuse to stay awake. 'Where are we going?' she whispered as Jake pulled on his clothes.

Jake creaked open the back door. He didn't look at the guinea-pigs as he passed, all seventeen of them, locked securely in their hutch, and like him, Tess kept her head down and hurried on. He led her past the chicken coop, through the wild and out on to the road.

'Jake . . .' she tried to call him back. It was cold and the sky was inky black.

'Come on.' He held out his hand, and they walked in silence down the hill, past the phone box and along beside the little stream. They passed the huge shadow of the yew tree, its gnarled trunk terrifying in the dark, the comforting daytime shelter of its branches wreathed round with ghosts. They walked quickly until they came out on to the golf-course. It didn't seem so dark up here, the green lawns glistening like a river, long and light, as if the bracken

215

that surrounded them was the riverbank. The bracken was all mulched and curled and dank, but underneath those rotting stalks tiny fronds of green were curled. Tess peered into the low dip of the valley to see the black outline of the Jenkinshaws' house. Jake began to wade towards it, cutting right through the undergrowth, leaving a battered path behind him in which Tess trod. When he reached the house he walked right up to the gate, and as he touched the latch the dog began to bark. Tess tugged at him and he stepped back. The dog growled and barked out one last yap. Then there was silence. They stood and looked up at the stars. They were thick up here, and brittle, and Tess wondered why they didn't come up here every night. 'Do you dare me?' Jake whispered, and he picked up a large stone. 'No,' Tess tried to say, but he'd already thrown it, hard, over the fence, smashing through a window by the Jenkinshaws' front door. The window splintered with such a sudden shock that it took a moment for the dog to bark.

Jake pulled Tess's hand and ran. They ran fast and blind, stumbling against stumps and roots, so that when eventually they were safe out by the phone box the legs of their trousers were stiff and wet. Quickly and silently they walked up the hill and without speaking they undressed and climbed back into bed.

Tess woke in the morning with her heart thudding in her chest, and when she slipped out to check her sheet she noticed that Jake had bundled his blanket up into a

cat-shaped hillock and he had it pressed against his
chest.

'I wander, I wander, a child in the night,
To give you a candle, to guide you with light.'

William led the children in a song as they trooped into the
kitchen to meet Eve. Francine was sitting there, the baby
in her arms, smiling, smooth and proud.

'Who's going to be the first to hold her?' William said
and Francine looked through the small crowd to search
out Tess.

Tess fixed her eyes on the baby. She did want to hold
her, but it didn't mean she was forgiving Francine for
what she'd done. Francine made her sit down in the
wooden armchair, nestled close into the stove for heat,
and when she was ready she lowered Eve into her arms.
Eve was wrapped in frothy lambswool with a tiny crocheted bonnet on her dark fluff head. She had a face like
a flower, and Tess could see immediately that she was
one of them. She didn't look like William, like any of his
three girls, and when Eve opened her eyes she looked just
like Francine.

First Doon, then Sandy, then Honour held the baby,
and then Melody put her against her shoulder and walked
around the room.

'Jake?' Francine tried to bring Eve to him, but when he

saw her coming he backed out of the room. 'Is everything all right?' Francine looked at William, and William patted her shoulder and smiled. 'He's been displaced, it's natural. He's feeling a bit raw, that's all.' Francine smiled at him, grateful for explaining, and gazed back down into the oval of Eve's face.

Now when Jake came home from school he climbed straight up on to his bunk. He lay flat on his back and looked up at the ceiling. Maybe, Tess thought, maybe William really did take Odin to a farm. But then if she asked, asked if they could visit, would William have to admit he'd put him down? She couldn't stand the thought of watching him fumble, searching round for an excuse, and then they'd know, they'd know for ever, that their Odin cat was dead.

'Oh Jake,' Tess said, but there was nothing she could say. She wrote instead.

Dear Dad,

Henrietta has started to lay eggs again. No one knows if she thought the chicks weren't really her own. Mum had her baby and she called it Eve which is lucky because I never really wanted to give Eliza back. Thank you for the book.

Love Tess

PS. Jake is in a bad mood. Will you –

But she didn't know what anyone could do so she crossed 'will you' out.

Victor had sent them a copy of his book. 'Well, who'd have thought it?' William was desperate to get his hands on it. 'The great master has produced something at last.' When he couldn't wait a moment longer he reached over and lifted it away from Jake. He turned it over, smoothed a finger down the spine, and examined the shiny grey grained cover. It was a photo of a woman's waist. 'Well,' he sighed, 'there's hope for us all.' He flipped the book open in the middle and began to read. '"His testicles were pimpled like the plucked skin of a chicken and hung too low between his legs."' William let out a little disbelieving gasp. '"They lacked buoyancy, and with a sudden nostalgia Cherry thought of the hot hard sack, the wide smooth shaft, the silky penis that she'd given up when she left Kim."' William let the book close with a snap.

'Flattering photo.' Francine leant over his shoulder, staring hard into Victor's handsome black-and-white face, biting her lip against laughter. 'William, you're blushing!'

'I guess I'm just provincial,' William said, and huffing, he took a slice of toast out of the tea towel and spread butter over the crust.

Francine was bending over Tess's bed, sniffing at the sheet.

'Tess,' she stood up, startled, catching one ear on the

corner of Jake's bunk, 'I was just wondering,' she looked at her with a hopeful smile, 'how you're getting on.'

Tess fixed her eyes on the door to Melody's room. 'I don't know what you mean.' Small grids of hurt were pressing on her chest.

Francine moved towards her, her arms wide open.

'I've got to do the chickens.' Tess backed away and she ran out of the room.

Tess squatted amongst the hens and tried to stroke them as they pecked. Their wings looked soft, but really they were bony and their beaks nicked the edges of her fingers as they tried to get the corn. The lump in her throat was hardening and, even though she fought them, tears dripped down on to the ground. Her mother had looked so startled, so miserable as if she didn't understand, and as Tess had run backwards to avoid her she'd noticed a dark stain of milk leaking through on to her mother's shirt. Tess fluffed her fingers and clucked for Henrietta. She was a bright brown bird and Tess loved her the best, but when she pressed her body against her it made her think of Odin and how he could bend into your side. He could talk to you, tell you what he thought, and even as she squatted there, she remembered how much he hated it when you cried. He'd mew and curl and nuzzle, pounce after you on to your bed, and now she and Jake had to lie alone in silence, with only each other to beg that they should stop.

Tess allowed herself to sleep now, but only so lightly

that she startled awake several times a night. She felt bruised and hardened, with all her energy used up during the night. Never again, she told herself, never again, as she jangled out of sleep. She had less time for Thor and Loki, and sometimes she almost forgot about Ragnarok. She wore the same nightdress, just to prove it, week after week, and she saw her mother watching her sadly when she went upstairs for songs.

Eve wasn't an easy baby. She fed and fed and then at night she cried. 'Listen, Francine,' William said as she walked Eve, howling, up and down. 'Would it be easier if I just took you off the rota?'

Francine didn't answer. Eve was crying too loudly in her ear.

'I'll take over her chores,' Melody smiled, and Tess noticed how she had a new way of pushing back her hair. Melody was helping William with his drama group and he'd appointed her assistant director for a production of *Job*. 'Why me? Why me? O Lord?' they laughed at each other across the table and his daughters always laughed too as if they knew it was a joke. Francine looked baffled and she tried to smile, and it made Tess sad she couldn't comfort her. She'd like to have sat close to her, laid her body along the warm length of her lap, but there was nothing she could do now she was no longer on her side.

William was organizing another trip to London. 'This

221

time,' he told Francine, 'I'll arrange things better.' Francine pulled up her shirt to quieten Eve with milk. 'I've put a great deal of thought into it all.' He was going to take his drama group to London on the last day of the Easter term. He'd take his three children with him and put them on the Edinburgh train. Honour was old enough to be in charge of the little ones until they reached Edinburgh, where Felicity could meet them herself. 'And then,' this was his masterstroke, 'I thought that maybe Victor would like to have Tess and Jake?'

'Victor? You mean for the night?'

'You need a break,' he urged her gently. 'You'll get a break. Melody's coming with me so you'll be completely alone.'

'I don't want to be completely alone.' Sudden fat tears had settled on her cheeks. 'Anyway, isn't Melody going back to America?'

'Not this time,' he smiled. 'Oh, come on.' He refused to be distracted. 'It'll be just what you need. Some time alone with the baby.' He edged his hand forward nervously to stroke Francine's cheek, and as she twisted away Eve lost hold of her nipple. The baby gasped and sucked at air, and then after a few desperate gurgles she began to scream.

Victor and Min were eating wine gums, leaning against the railing as the passengers streamed by. 'Hey,' they waved and Jake began to run. Tess followed him, clinging to his coat. 'Hello,' said Victor, and Min offered them both a sweet.

It was strange to see Jake shy. He sat in the back of the taxi and smiled down at his feet. 'We thought we'd go to Min's,' Victor said and the taxi weaved and turned and bounced them on its way.

Min lived in a narrow house that backed on to a canal. The water was dark brown and lifeless, long slicks of oil snaked along the edge. There were several other doors behind Min's front door and she opened one so narrow Victor had to turn his shoulders sideways to get through. The first room was a bathroom, and instead of carrying on up to the next landing Min trooped them all inside. 'Do you want to see my eels?' Her pale eyes danced with light, and Tess and Jake stepped forward to see. The eels lay in the bottom of Min's bath, overlapping like the slimy inner-tubes of tyres, their narrow heads slit through with thin black mouths. The water around them was silted up and murky, with dark rings around the bath where slowly the level had gone down. 'Water's getting a bit low,' Min said and she turned on the cold tap. The eels rippled, the movement slithering along the whole length of their tails so that Tess involuntarily stepped back on to her father's shoe. 'They're alive!' Jake said, and Tess had a sudden image of pie and mash and eel, Min cutting the thick meat with her fork.

Jake craned further in to see. 'What happens when you

have a bath?' But Min had headed off to the next landing, twittering and tutting, making small kissing noises with her lips. 'There you are!' She stooped down and picked up a small hairy animal and pressed it against her neck. A long pink tail trailed down towards her waist.

'A rat?' Jake was impressed. 'Can I hold it?'

'He's called Sally,' Min said, passing him over. 'I thought he was a girl.'

'I don't know how,' Victor laughed. 'Look at the size of his balls.'

'When he was a baby.' Min glared with such ferocity that Victor cowered in mock alarm.

Sally was white, with black uneven patches like a Fresian cow. His whiskers were long and spiky and there was a brightness in the happy twitching of his nose. 'He's very intelligent,' Min told them, 'and extremely clean.'

'Yes, and if you don't get up at seven to feed him, he runs over your head.'

'So?' Min threw Victor another ice-cold look.

'I'd love that,' Jake said.

Min made them both ham sandwiches and gave them peach juice so thick it was like soup. Victor watched her, following her every movement with narrow, passionate eyes, but whatever it was he'd said or done Min wasn't ready to forgive him. Once or twice she kicked him sharply as she passed, and although he flinched he didn't say a word. Tess felt alarmed for him. He'd never been so interested in Georgina, although Georgina never kicked him or minded anything he said. But then she had attacked his car. Tess wondered if the car was mended, or if each time the blue was layered on, the blue over the special blue, Georgina came back with the full moon and scraped it off.

Min took them to an enormous pet shop. The owner nodded at Min and smiled, and even though he was a small fair man with a pocked face like a gerbil, Victor still narrowed his eyes menacingly at him, and while they shouldered their way past birds and mice and tanks of tropical fish he put one hand on the back of Min's white neck. Min shook him off, but softly, and when they reached the rack of cages for the rats she reached behind her for his hand. The rats were mostly babies and all of them were black and white. 'They're all relations of Sally's,' Min said, and she took Sally from underneath her jumper and let him swap whiskery kisses with his friends.

That night they slept at Min's. One on each of her battered sofas with dusty rugs and bedspreads pulled up to their chins. In the room above they could hear the creak of floorboards and the murmur of their father, deep and low and hushed, with sudden flips and mewls from Min. Tess woke in the unfamiliar dark to hear Victor's footsteps shuffling down the stairs and then descending, deeper, past the bathroom and out through the two sets of doors on to the street.

'Where's Dad?' Jake asked in the morning, and Tess rolled over sleepily and stretched. 'He's gone.'

It was nice alone with Min. She brought them glasses of fruit juice on their sofas and let them throw crumbs for Sally, forcing him to leap from one sofa to the next. Min played records for them. Old black husky voices singing stories full of jokes.

Say up in Harlem got a table for two
There were four of us. Me, your big feet and you.

It was only when Tess got up to dance she remembered that she hadn't even thought to check her bed. Her heart stopped for a moment, and then when she realized that she was warm and dry she felt washed over with such a sense of peace that she danced like a crazy girl right in the centre of the room.

Your feet's too big,
Don't want you 'cause your feet's too big,
Can't use you 'cause your feet's too big,
I really hate you 'cause you feet's too big.

'Yes sir!' Jake and Min whooped in admiration and

Tess spun around, stamping and spinning, bunching up her long white nightdress like a rose.

When they'd run out of peach juice and washed their hands and faces in the sink beside the eels they went out to meet Victor.

'He likes to work at night,' Min told them, and when they rang his bell he came down to answer it, startled as if he'd been caught out of a trance.

'Breakfast,' Min told him, clapping him gently on the ear, 'or would you like Sally to run over your head?'

Victor clasped Min to him and pressed her to his chest, his eyes closed tight as if he was in pain, and Tess understood he had to rush in at the tender moments or he'd get nothing at all.

'Where to?' Victor loosened his hold, and Min said she needed meat.

They sat in a deserted cafe and ate kebabs on a thick bed of rice. 'We don't have to tell William,' Jake whispered to Tess as she stared at a dribble of pink blood, and urged on by Min and Victor, she bit into the meat.

Victor took them to a bookshop. It was Sunday so they had to hammer on the door. 'Ralph,' Min shouted, cupping her hands round her mouth.

'His name's Wilf, you complete idiot,' Victor told her and they leant against the door, their shoulders shaking as they laughed.

'Wilf!' Min, Jake and Tess all called together, and Victor threw a cigarette packet that missed the window and bounced back at him off the wall.

Eventually the shop door was pulled open. Tess stepped back, expecting there to be a row, but Wilf was smiling. 'What's all this?' He was a round man with a huge bobbled jumper and trousers that hung low on his hips.

'We need books,' Victor told him and they walked through into his shop. Wilf glanced suspiciously at Tess and Jake. 'They're not – it seems so unlikely somehow – his children?'

Min peered at shelves and shrugged her shoulders as if she wasn't the one to be giving things away.

Jake wanted a comic. Spiderman or Batman. Tess worried in case it was a signal to the others that he couldn't read. 'We don't sell comics here,' Wilf said, 'but I'll tell you what, I've got some of my own somewhere.' He smiled at Jake. 'Good choice. A man of taste. Don't want to be doing with all that literature,' and he thundered off upstairs.

It was evening when they caught their train. Min had bought them each a present. A book for Tess about a girl who really did grow up in the wild. *Little House on the Prairie*, Tess mouthed and she stroked the smooth spine of the book. For Jake she had a rat. 'He's Sally's great-great-grandson.' The rat was black and white with tiny

228

twinkling eyes. His body was warm and rippling as he ran along Jake's arm.

'I'll call him Nin,' Jake said, and he kissed him on the nose. 'Can we come and visit again soon?' Jake stood close against his father, measuring his height against Victor's arm.

Victor shuffled his feet. 'Well, I'm not sure. You see, I'm going to America. I'll be travelling around, talking about my book . . . giving lectures.' He looked uncomfortable. 'I'll be a sort of freak show,' he decided, and that seemed to cheer him up. 'At the moment I don't know when I'll be back.'

Jake stood very still. 'Oh,' he said, and for a moment Tess thought he was going to cry. 'Shhh,' he said instead to Nin, and he nudged him into the safety of his sleeve. Without looking round he climbed on to the train.

'Will you be going too?' Tess leant out of the window, but Min just raised the perfect arches of her eyebrows and kicked Victor on the shin.

'Bye then, bye.' The train was moving off. 'Jake,' she urged, when he didn't wave, but Jake sat with his back to London. 'Bye.' She tried to call for both of them, and she waved until they were gone.

How would they bear it, Tess thought, if the next time they went to London their father wasn't there. If there was no peach juice or dancing, no Sally, no Min. She sat facing Jake and looked out of the window, watching for the countryside to start, and soon after Clapham

Junction the small back gardens turned from grey to green, the fire escapes were phased away, and hedges grew instead of wire.

'Go on, then.' Jake sat slumped in his seat. 'Tell me one of those disgusting stories. I don't mind.'

Tess closed her eyes. She could see Mr Paul standing breathless at the front of their class and she shivered with the strange chill that he created when he told them how Loki had met his end. He'd been so heartless and so full of tricks that all the gods agreed that he had sealed his fate. They'd tied him up with the entrails of his own bastard son, and when he was tied tight, they'd dragged him into a cave and placed him under a poisonous snake. The snake dripped venom on to his face and as it splashed on him he writhed in pain. But his wife, his ever faithful wife Sigyn, had tried to help him. She'd stood over him, collecting the poison in a bowl, so that it was only when she had to step aside to empty it that the poison burnt his face. Loki and Sigyn waited in that cave. They waited for the end. And the only end there was, was Ragnarok.

Jake had found a peanut in his pocket, and he was feeding it to Nin. It was a peanut that had been there for some time. Nin gnawed at it with his teeth as if it was a boulder, scratching and scratching until he fell asleep. Jake curled him into his jumper, and as he listened to Tess's stories he watched the rat's tiny nostrils quiver happily in his dreams.

★

William sat in Soho in the bar where he'd seen Victor. The chairs were silver slatted metal and were as light as tin. He looked across at Melody and smiled. It's nice being on this side of the street, he thought, and he looked over at the drabness of the dark green pizzeria where a mermaid was painted, bare breasted, on one wall. Now he was here in the sunshine, drinking real Italian coffee in tiny overpriced cups. He moved his chair towards Melody so that it clinked as it overlapped with hers. Melody looked up and smiled sleepily. The night before he'd told his other students he was staying behind to escort Melody to her train. She was off to stay with friends, he said, in Walton-on-the-Naze.

'You think they believed you?' Melody twirled her arms to show she didn't care.

'No, but all the same.' He had stood at the barrier, counting his students as they got on the train, reminding himself they were perfectly capable of getting back to East Grinstead alone. 'All the same it's best to be careful about these things.'

'You old fool,' she laughed. 'They know, they know.'

William was irritated. 'Not so old.' But when Melody ran off through the thinning station, he chased after her and caught her round the waist. They wandered along the broad white streets of Pimlico, where he'd heard it was always possible to get a room. But the room they found was small and dank and dismal and it had taken too long to find. William felt tired. More tired than he wanted to admit. A tube of fluorescent lighting was flickering in the hall and he could hear the toilet flushing. 'That wretched light.' He shook his head and Melody stood by the window looking out as if she was made of new white stone. He had to stop himself from commenting on the bedspread, a faded cotton cover with small ridges of cloth that wriggled along it like small worms. His bare feet were sticky on the carpet and when he came back from using the bathroom, Melody was already in the bed. He could see her pearly shoulders rising up out of the minced-mutton quilt and in desperation he knelt down on the floor. 'I bet you didn't know I could do this.' He began to raise himself into a headstand, his two hands flat on the floor, and as he rose up he could see Melody, her face superior and upside down. 'And this!' He stretched his long legs upwards and then, crossing them at the knee, he folded his feet into the lotus position, one foot under each thigh. 'It's a rare achievement for a man,' he told her but he could no longer see Melody through the pain. His eyes stung, the joints in his ankles and his knees felt ready to snap, and quickly, before he started screaming, he crashed against the cupboard to get down. His feet were stuck, trapped under the muscle of each thigh, and he had to roll into a sitting position and unbend them with his hands. 'Ahhh,' he moaned as he massaged his legs, his head numb from pressing into the floor, and by the time he climbed into bed beside Melody she'd fallen asleep, her face towards the wall. God, he thought, irritated and relieved, now we'll have to spend another night together, and he remembered the manageress of the hotel telling them their room must be vacated by eight.

Francine was driving William's van. It came heaving round the station forecourt and pulled up beside the bus stop with a screech. Eve was in her carry cot, strapped to the front seat, and when Francine got out her face was streaked with tears. 'Get in, get in.' She unstrapped Eve and put her into Tess's arms.

'What is it, Mum?' Tess asked, forgetting that she wasn't supposed to be her friend, and she noticed Francine was wearing her old clothes again, her pale knitted jumper and her jeans. Tess climbed into the front with Eve and propped her up on her lap. She kissed the downy top of her head and danced with her small hands.

'It's William.' Francine slammed the door. 'I don't know where he is. The others, they all came back last night, but when I came to the station to collect William, he just wasn't here. I had to pretend that I'd forgotten, make out that because of the baby, my brain had unravelled into mush. Of course he was busy taking Melody to her train. Of course. But I could see them, the parents of all those hideous teenagers, looking at me as if I was a fool.' Francine started to cry. She flicked the wipers on as if it was the rain. 'I thought maybe, maybe he was on the train with you?'

'No,' Jake said.

'Anyway,' Francine wiped her nose. She turned to them and tried to smile. 'Anyway, did you have an all right time?'

'Yes,' they both said. And Tess thought how nice it was that they were friends again.

The next day William walked up the ramp with a large carrier bag swinging from his arm. The bag said Foyles, and when Francine ran in to question him he turned the bag upside down and let a stream of books spill out on to the table. Francine looked round. 'Where's Melody?'

'Melody? She's gone to stay with friends. I told you I'd arrange it so you had a few days off.' William was whistling a silly tune as he arranged the books into three piles.

Francine was pale and breathless, battling with tears. 'How could you do this to me?' She stood beside him, very quiet and still. 'After everything you've said about trust. About honesty and guilt.'

William looked over at her perplexed. His eyebrows were wrinkled just like Spotless. 'I know what I've got for you,' he smiled, and he handed her a book. As she stretched out for it, he held her wrist. 'Believe me, Francine. Please?'

'*Zen and the Art of Motorcycle Maintenance.*' Francine read the title, and as she tried not to smile thick tears fell on to the cover. 'You bastard.' She was smiling and crying now. 'You bastard.' But she held on to the book.

★

Jake made a cage for Nin. 'You'll be safe from Pale Face in here,' he told him, and he padlocked the rat in. He kept the key to the padlock on his belt, and when he slept he put it under his pillow. 'He'll have to kill me first to get at it,' he said, narrowing his eyes. But mostly Jake let Nin sit on his shoulder, or lie like a hammock in the elbow of his sleeve. 'Where do you think we'll move to next, now the truth is out about Wooden Willy and Perpetual Love?' Nin ran over his hands, and Jake moved them faster and faster so that Nin looked like he was climbing stairs.

Tess didn't know. If they moved, what would happen to the chickens and the badminton, the fancy-dress clothes and William's songs? 'Will he want to fight for custody of Eve?' Tess asked, alarmed, and Jake laughed. He laughed and laughed, his mouth wide open, until Tess turned away from the noise. She remembered her mother once saying to Mrs Bremmer as she measured out food at the biodynamic farm, talking when she thought Tess wasn't there, and she was saying that no one ever wanted to get hold of *her* children. No one really wanted anything to do with them at all. They'd talked then about William being such a fantastic father, and how unusual it was for a man to get sole custody of three girls. 'Oh yes,' Mrs Bremmer's eyes had swelled wide with rumours and she'd told Francine that apparently he'd done everything he could to sway the judge. He'd claimed Felicity was a sex-mad, drug-addicted lesbian. He'd even found some man from her karate class to give evidence against her in court. 'No,' Francine had shaken her head, appalled, but on the way home she'd realized she'd forgotten millet, wheatgerm and dried bananas, and she'd pulled the van over and sat for a long time on the verge.

Jake was still laughing. 'No,' he spluttered eventually, 'he won't want Eve. Of course he won't.'

And suddenly Tess hoped that they would move. 'Me, you, Mum and Eve,' she said. 'We'll live in a house by the railway.' Railway cottage. She'd seen it once on one of Jake's sponsored walks. 'We'll plant a rose for each of us around the door.'

'And Nin.' Jake sounded hurt. 'Don't forget about a rose for Nin.'

But Francine was forgiving him. She'd held out for two days and then William had locked himself in his workshop and said he wasn't to be disturbed. All day they'd waited and wondered, and then at suppertime he reappeared with a little seat for Eve. It had her name carved on one side and two handles to carry it along. It was a seat like a bed with two wooden sloping sides so that Eve could lie in comfort wrapped up in a rug.

Eve was a smooth and easy baby now. She cooed and smiled a sweet, curling smile when you looked into her face. Tess couldn't resist her. She dangled necklaces for her, shook tiny bells, and as she bent over her she blew kisses into the tiny hidden creases of her neck.

The next morning William set Eve's seat out in the garden and settled her there to watch while he helped Francine dib new seeds into the ground. They were planting their summer vegetables – carrots, lettuce, kale and spinach – and as they worked Francine's face was soft with smiles. She looked more beautiful than ever in her old narrow clothes, and Tess saw how her ankles were turned and elegant again. At night William baked apples with ginger, butter and brown sugar, he made elderflower fritters and bananas roasted in their skins, and when with a flourish he presented them to her, Francine blushed and shook her head.

Jake didn't speak. He sat glum and silent and as soon as supper was over he shut himself in his room.

'I hear you've got a new pet.' William tried to draw him out. 'Where've you been hiding her?'

'Him,' Jake said. He stroked Nin's tail as it hung like a lapel against his shirt.

William started. 'Isn't it rather unhygienic to eat supper in the company of a rat?' He looked at Francine. 'Has he washed his hands?'

'He's tame,' Jake told him. 'Nin's very intelligent and very clean.'

'That's right.' Francine looked straight at William, as if they'd come to some agreement over Jake. William bent back over his food.

'But in future,' he couldn't resist one more word, 'not at suppertime, do you understand?'

Jake looked towards Francine to intercede, but Francine just shook her head and shrugged.

At bedtime, instead of singing songs, William sat in the empty fireplace and read poems from an anthology of Scottish verse. The poems thrilled Francine and sent Eve straight to sleep, and they sat there like a holy picture, the three of them, draped round with a quilt.

The night the Strachan girls came back Tess woke up to find Jake gone. She could hear Nin in his cage, snuffling and snoring, and there was a flat black space where Jake usually lay.

Tess crept out of bed. 'Jake?' she whispered through the house, but she knew that he had gone. She stood on the back step and waited and when light started showing in the sky, she went back to bed. Melody had come back too the day before. She'd walked up from the bus-stop and the first thing she'd seen when she walked into The Wild was William digging in potatoes with Eve strapped to his back. Melody had stood there, all sleek and coppery in a see-through cheesecloth shirt, and when William had stopped and stretched and leant over to laugh at something Francine said, Melody had slammed straight into her room. A moment later William came after her. He'd got rid of Eve but his hands were thick with mud. He lowered his head as he walked through Tess and Jake's room and he'd stood there blushing as he waited for Melody to let him in.

'It's proof,' Jake whispered, standing with his ear to the door. 'It's proof that he's a cheat.' His chest was heaving. 'If he doesn't come out soon,' he said, 'I'll . . . I'll.' But he didn't know what he'd do.

That night at supper Melody had two dark handprints on her shirt. They had stained the thin cloth brown and little grits of earth clung to her back. 'How was Walton-on-the-Naze?' Francine asked her. She was running between the table and the stove, with the baby propped up on one shoulder. 'Honour, get that sauce before it burns.'

Melody was smiling again. 'Fine,' she said. 'Just fine.'

'Jake.' Tess woke up with a start, remembering that he'd gone.

'Jake.' But he was there, lying sleeping with his face into the pillow, one hand dangling over the edge of his bunk.

'Where were you?' she asked.

'Nowhere.' He sat up, bright-eyed suddenly and awake. 'Nowhere at all.'

He looked unusually happy as he pulled on his clothes, and Tess noticed there were burs on his jumper and the hems of his trousers were wet. At breakfast, for the first time ever, he offered to say Grace.

'Before the flour the mill,
Before the mill the grain,
Before the grain, the sun, the earth, the rain.
The beauty of God's will.'

It was William's favourite Grace. I'm winning him round. I knew I would. Patience. Patience. He smiled with pleasure at Jake and thought how unfair it was that the prodigal son meant more than all the rest.

'Right,' he said. 'Time for school.' And as he swung his bag into the van, he noticed Melody was wearing a black bra under her cheesecloth shirt.

'Winter had lost its heart,' Tess wrote in her mainlesson book. 'Every day the stallions Arvak and Alsvid rose earlier to haul the Sun's chariot across the sky.'

She was nervous that the Norse Myths were going to end. 'Does there have to be the battle of Ragnarok?' she asked Mr Paul, sidling close in to him as he chalked a picture of the shape-shifting god.

'Don't worry,' he told her, filling in every corner of the board.

'It won't come until you're ready.' He told them the story of how Loki caught an otter, just before he was caught himself, and in the otter's mouth there was a fish. But the otter turned out to be someone's brother, someone's son, and soon Loki and his friends Odin and

Honir were bound hand and foot for killing the otter, who was just a fisherman in disguise.

Tess thought through the details of this story as she pulled weeds out of her garden. If they weren't going to be moving after all, she'd better set to work on her plot of land. She had a trowel and she was digging up the earth. And then out of the stillness, over the garden wall, there came the crash and echo of a shot. It rippled out just like the crack of marksmen shooting grouse, but this time it was right behind the house. Tess straightened up and the trowel fell on to the ground. It bounced and caught her foot, and then she heard the workshop door slam open and she saw Honour running out. She was running fast, her face all out of focus. 'Daddy?' she called, and there was pure terror in her voice. 'Where are you, Daddy?' Doon and Sandy had streamed out of the house. They darted around like midges and then with Honour in the lead they raced through into the wild. Tess followed. 'William, where are you?' She felt sick in each part of her body and she didn't care as the branches caught her arms.

William was standing on the caravan's steps, the echo of the shot still hanging in the air. 'I'm here.' His face was white and sickly and he stood very still as they tried to gather round.

Jake was lying on the caravan floor. Blood seeped out from under him, spreading along the green gloss boards, soaking into the wood. It's going, Tess thought, his blood is going and we'll never get it back.

'Stand back, the lot of you!' William swallowed hard, and Tess saw he had a dark wood rifle in his hand.

'What is it?' Francine was standing in her orange wrap-around skirt. Her eyes were speckled, olive, and they were bursting out with fear.

'Just go next door and call an ambulance,' William told her and Tess worried that Major Darlby might only let her use the phone on condition she clean up the spare van. He'd been complaining about it, pushed so close in to his wall, saying all winter it was a disgrace, covered in graffiti, collecting moulding leaves. Francine moved towards Jake, her arms flailing to get near. 'Hurry!' William shouted at her then. 'There's been an accident here.'

But the Darlbys must have let Francine in because soon the ambulance arrived, and then straight afterwards a police car with its siren flashing, soundless and blue. There was a policewoman and the policeman who'd come to warn them that Spotless might have to be put down. The ambulancemen peeled away the shirt William had used to staunch Jake's blood and they wrapped him in a blanket. Tess watched in case they covered up Jake's head. She started forward, wanting to go with him, wanting to catch hold of his white hand hanging from the stretcher, but Francine was already in the ambulance, holding Eve against her, kneeling on the floor to stroke Jake's face. She didn't look around as the heavy doors were pushed shut after them. She just knelt on the floor beside the stretcher as if she might never get up again.

'We'd like you to come with us.' The policeman had hold of William's bare arm, and Tess watched as, very carefully, he eased the gun out of his hand. It had a silver ring around its nose and its dark wood handle shone.

'No.' William tried to pull away and Tess saw that the scar curled over his stomach had turned an angry red. There were small flecks of blood on his shoulders and a smear across his nose. The policewoman tried to drape a blanket over him, but he pushed it off.

'You don't need me,' William explained, but the policeman strengthened his hold. 'It was all an accident. I was trying to get the gun away from him. "Shoot me if you like," I said, "but you'll wreck the rest of your life." And then – and then, I don't know how it happened, the gun went off.'

'Is there anyone to keep an eye on all these children?' The policewoman didn't seem to be listening to what he said.

'Yes.' Melody was standing by the gate. 'I'll look after them.' Her eyes were wide and blue and her hair was frizzing at the ends. Whatever she had to do to straighten it had slipped her mind. The children stood back a little as William got into the car. It was parked right by the side gate on the road, and William had to bend his knees to fit into the back.

'I'll be home soon.' He looked at his daughters and then he looked at Tess. 'It'll be all right, you'll see.' He smiled at her, crinkling his eyes in that special way, but although it was what she'd waited for, hoped for every day for nearly two years, now it was too late. She saw suddenly that Jake was right. William's nose was bulbous and his arms above the elbows were too white. His hair was cut in a pudding bowl and you could see the pink skin of his scalp where it parted at the top. Tess didn't even nod. She shrank away from him and walked back into the house.

Class Five were to perform a Midsummer Pageant on the theme of Ragnarok. Everyone stretched up their hands for a part. There were the nine worlds, the gods, the giants, the men, the dwarves, the birds and the beasts.

'An axe age, a sword age, shields will be gashed. There will be a wind age and a wolf age before the world is wrecked.' Mr Paul held on to the edge of his desk and told them how a wolf seized the sun between his jaws and swallowed her. How the moon was mangled and the stars vanished from the sky.

Finally, finally, they were doing the battle of Ragnarok and Tess could see, for the first time, that it wasn't real.

Dear Dad,

Mr Paul's brother-in-law says we can stay in this flat. It's quite near the hospital. It's got a kitchen that's so small you have to eat your meals sitting on the bed, and when

Jake gets better he can make us cheese on toast for breakfast. Now Mum knows it's true about Melody she says we can stay here as long as we want. The really silly thing about Ragnarok is that some men and gods get left over and find a bit of the world that isn't destroyed and everything starts up again. I wish I'd known that. Lif and Lifthrasir have children, and their children have children, and on and on.

Are you back from America yet? I wish you were.

Love Tess

Tess went back to The Wild to collect Jake's rat. She couldn't take the chickens but she didn't mind. Nin was sitting in their room, exactly like they'd left him, except Doon had been feeding him and letting him out to run. There was no one in the house, and Tess felt guilty, as if she was breaking in. The door to Melody's room was wide open and when she looked inside there was nothing there. The bed was stripped, the little desk was clear, and the flowered curtains Francine had made were drawn across the window.

Tess tiptoed back through the kitchen and looked at everything as if it wasn't hers. She noticed the rota was hanging from one pin. 'Go placidly amid the noise and haste . . .' She tried not to read *The Desiderata* and then she heard a shuffle on the stairs. It was William. He was standing by the door wearing the socks she'd knitted for him. 'They laid me off,' he told her. His trousers looked too short, as if they'd shrunk in a hot wash, and they were pulled too tight up by his crotch. He'd been held in the police station for a whole night and a day, and the police had only let him out when Mr Jenkinshaw had driven over to identify his gun.

Tess held tight on to the handle of Nin's cage. She wished William would say something so that she could go. He was looking at her too hard. Eventually he swallowed. 'I did love your Mummy, you know.' Tess looked at his feet. The socks looked ridiculously stripy, the wool all stretched like slippers ready to be thrown away. She wondered if he expected her to cry, to ask him to jump into his van and drive over and beg Francine to stay.

'Bye then.' She lifted Nin's cage into her arms, and holding it tight like a basket she ran as fast as she could out of the side gate and down the hill. She ran past the phone box and the shop, and only stopped when she reached the little bus shelter where a bus stopped eleven minutes before or after each alternate hour. I don't believe you, I don't believe you, I don't believe you. It took a while for her breathing to calm down, and by the time the bus finally arrived, its double-decker green lopsided on the narrow road, she felt light-hearted and glad.

Tess liked being high up. She could twist down from the top bunk and watch Jake as he talked to her, all smooth

246

and peaceful in the dark. He was getting better but he was still too weak to climb. It was nice listening to stories from up here, and now Jake was on the bottom bunk he even told her tiny tempting snippets about life in Ancient Egyptian times. He told her about Isis and Osiris and the Underworld through which you had to pass for seven days. It was what he had been learning about at school the week that he'd been shot.

'Did you just mean to frighten him with that gun?' Tess asked. She'd been waiting to ask Jake this until he was out of hospital. He'd only missed being paralysed by a fraction of an inch, and there was going to be a scar.

'No,' he said. 'I meant to kill him.'

Tess tried to swipe him with her arm, but Jake was laughing.

Even Francine liked living in this tiny flat. It was the first time they'd been able to shut the door and be alone. 'So much for communal living,' she said.

Nin liked it particularly. It meant he didn't have to be locked in his cage but could run wherever he wanted through the rooms. He made a bed for himself in a box of Francine's papers and he liked to jump straight out of there when Jake called his name.

Tess looked up at the ceiling. She thought of William's strong hands and his honeyed hair, falling low over his guitar.

'Do you miss him?' Jake asked as if he could read her

mind, and he used the end of his crutch to prod her through the bed.

'You mean William?' They hardly ever said his name. Tess tried to stretch her arms up to the ceiling. There was bobbled wood-chip wallpaper to make the room look warm. 'No,' she said, and she thought how much she'd ached for him to like her. 'No I don't.' And she realized it was true.